CW01429838

TABLE OF CONTENTS

About This book	v
Over the Falls Without A Barrel	1
Deadly Dunes	16
The Man in Seat 13B	38
California Adventure	50
Destined for Sandestin	72
A Christmas Caper	90
Read more Sassy Senior Sleuths Mysteries	103
About the Author Kathryn Mykel	104
About the Author P.C. James	106

ABOUT THIS BOOK

Travel can be murder. Can Miss Riddell and Nona catch the villains before they become victims?
Travel forward from the Miss Riddell series to the twenty-first century with the demure Miss Pauline Riddell as she befriends a strangely lovable, fly-by-the-seat-of-her-pants amateur sleuth, named Gretta Galia aka Nona. Together, the two sixty-five year-old travel companions visit tourist destinations around the United States.

These stories move forward twenty years from the Miss Riddell Series by P.C. James and backward in time twenty years from Sewing Suspicion Quilting Cozy Mysteries by Kathryn Mykel. Approximating the setting to be between 2000-2005.

Join us in the Adventures of Pauline and Nona Facebook group:

https://www.facebook.com/groups/paulineandnona/

From the creative writers: P.C. James, author of the Best-Selling Miss Riddell Cozy Mystery Series and Kathryn Mykel, Award-Winning author of Best-Selling Sewing Suspicion, Quilting Cozy Mystery.

1

OVER THE FALLS WITHOUT A BARREL

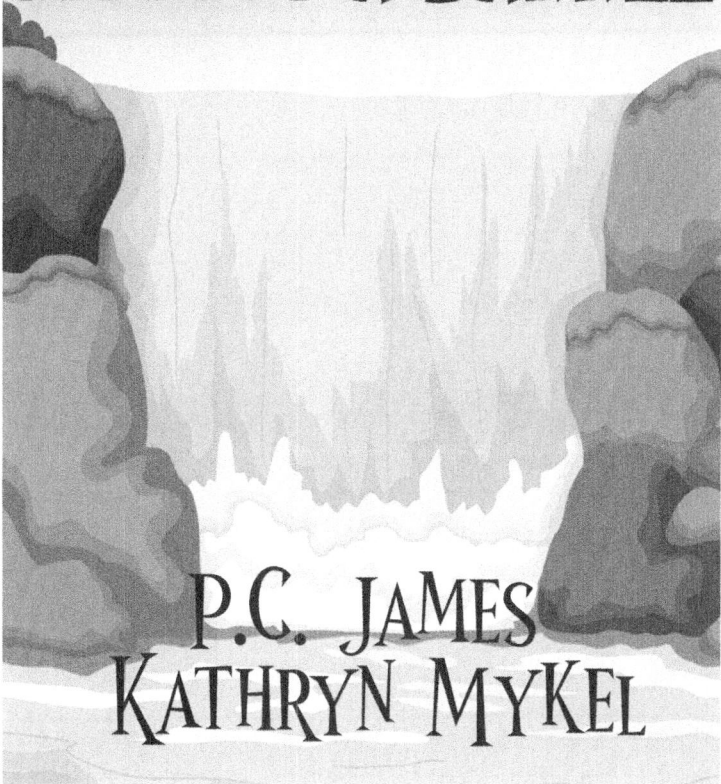

P.C. JAMES
KATHRYN MYKEL

OVER THE FALLS WITHOUT A BARREL

Mini Mystery #1

Pauline Riddell looked around the Niagara Falls Winery's kitchen, where she was taking part in a cooking and wine event, and surveyed her fellow travelers. Mainly middle-aged women and a few couples, most of whom seemed to know each other. A group from a wine club from just over the border in New York, she guessed. The chef, Chef Corsair, who was to be their teacher for the meal they were to prepare, had not appeared, and the worried owner of the winery had raced off to find him, leaving the group to chatter among themselves.

"You with them?" a woman seated near Pauline of a similar age asked, gesturing at the group, which was now developing ever wilder stories about the chef and the wine cellar.

"No," Pauline said. "Though it might be nice to have someone to share the experience with. Are you here alone?"

"There was to be two of us, but Betty got sick. For the price I paid for this view," she swept her hand towards the floor-to-ceiling windows, "I wasn't missing this for anything. I can't wait to meet the chef. I read an article that he is about to land an American TV deal. Is he some kind of Canadian celebrity?"

"Not that I am aware." Pauline frowned. "I was supposed to have a companion also, but like you, that fell through. We could learn together," she continued, making a space on the countertop so the woman could place her utensils nearby.

When the move from the other prep station was complete, Pauline turned to her new friend and held out her hand and said, "I am Pauline, Pauline Riddell." The woman shook her hand with a surprisingly firm grip.

"Gretta Galia," the woman said, "though everyone calls me 'Nona.'"

"Pleased to meet you, Nona," Pauline said. "Now we just need the return of our host and his chef, and we are set to make *Poulet Bonne Femme*, 'the easy way.'"

"Poulet a la Bonne Femme," Nona replied in a dreadful French accent.

They had only just stopped speaking when the host returned to the kitchen. His face was white, and his hands shook as he spoke. "Ladies and gentlemen, there's been a horrible accident. The chef is dead. An ambulance and the police are on their way. The police have asked that no one leave until they have talked to us all."

The murmuring that had begun the moment he said 'accident' now broke into his halting speech.

"How long will that be?" a loud voice asked, and there was a considerable rumble of agreement.

"I'm sure they won't keep you long," the winery owner said desperately. "After all, none of you actually met the chef, so you could have played no part in his death."

"Exactly," the loud man said. "We don't need to be here. It will take all day if the police interview us all."

Fortunately for the winery owner, the wail of sirens arriving in the parking lot outside signaled an end to this attempt to escape. *But why would this man be so keen to get away?* Pauline and Nona exchanged looks.

"I bet he's in on it," Nona whispered.

Pauline smiled. "If it is an accident," she said, "he is likely not *in on it.*"

"If it was an accident, the police wouldn't want to talk to us all," Nona said. "No, he's in on it, and I'll prove it."

"We should leave it to the police," Pauline whispered.

"No way," Nona said. "We're in the thick of it now." She clapped and rubbed her hands together. "Besides, I have experience in this kind of thing, and my experience says Loud Guy is guilty."

Pauline considered briefly whether she wanted to be mixed up in this, but her almost-made-decision not to was dashed when the police detective who walked into the kitchen spotted her at once and said, "Why, Miss Riddell. How do you turn up whenever there's a murder to solve?"

"I am here to learn about wine and cooking, Detective Smith," Pauline said, "and I understood this was an accident."

"With the best hope in the world, someone might think that," the detective said. "But we can talk later. Now," he continued, looking at the assembled group, "ladies and gentlemen, my officers will be asking you . . ."

"So you solve crimes too," Nona said, excitedly fluttering her eyelashes. "We'll tag-team this one and show that youngster how it's done."

Pauline was involved now, whether she liked it or not, Pauline said, "Very well, I suggest we go with your nose and investigate that loud guy first. I hope it is him because I do not like him."

ONCE THE GROUP was allowed to leave, after being questioned, Nona and Pauline received a clipped warning from the detective to stay out of the investigation.

"Where are you staying?" Nona asked. "I'm at the Embassy Suites."

"Yes, as am I," Pauline replied, ushering Nona towards the shuttle. "We can ride the shuttle back together and discuss what we saw at that crime scene."

Taking seats next to one another, the two women chatted during the ride from the vineyard to the Embassy Suites. In the noontime traffic they had a good fifteen minutes to get to know one another.

Nona, born and raised in Massachusetts, resided on Spruce Street, in Salem. Nicknamed Nona for her no-nonsense personality, though in her aging years she had become wild and free, while also being reserved and secretive about her past. She was well dressed, well manicured—nearly perfectly put together. With wavy blonde hair, she wore matching shirt/pant outfits. She'd been widowed by war at a young age, and had one son, who was now a mayor.

Originally from England, Pauline now lived in Canada, the Toronto area. She was known as Miss Riddell in the sleuthing world, and Pauline to friends and few remaining family. Her fiancé had been killed in the Korean War, and she'd never married after. She had been employed for many years in finance, but was now retired and traveling to see the world, though she had also traveled for work earlier in her life. Pauline was a conscientious churchgoer and personally straitlaced, though she wasn't shocked by those who weren't. When she realized sleuthing was her future, she trained in self-defense and firearms.

"Let's get a bite to eat when we get to the hotel," Nona remarked. "I am famished. The least they could have done was feed us!"

"I was amazed by how quickly the situation went from 'horrible accident' to 'murder.'"

"Well, he didn't go over the falls in a barrel." Nona chortled.

"You mentioned you have 'experience'? Were you in law enforcement or . . .?" Pauline asked, leaving it open-ended, hoping for more information from her traveling companion, whom she'd only known for a few hours.

"Ah, let's just say I saw plenty of action in my younger years." Nona winked and stepped out of the shuttle van. "You? Are you a detective or private investigator?" she asked of Pauline, exiting behind her.

"Sleuth. And I know my way around a crime scene," Pauline replied.

"Speaking of which, will your connection to that detective get us access?"

"Doubtful. You heard him. *Stay out of it, ladies.*" Pauline gave a fair impression of the young detective.

THE TWO WOMEN were quickly seated in the hotel restaurant, for lunch. "Well, at least we get that dish after all." Nona pointed to the Poulet Bonne Femme listed on the menu.

"Let us go over what we know." Pauline placed her order with the server.

"A group of strangers at a restaurant and the chef turns up . . ." Nona made a croaking noise and lolled her head to the side, dramatically.

"A loudmouthed man, eager to flee the scene before the police arrive," Pauline continued, ignoring her new friend's theatrics. "I believe I overheard him say he was friends with the chef's wife?"

"Well, that is a classic." Nona brimmed with pride. "Love affair turned deadly."

"I believe it is too early to make that assumption. How about the chef?" Pauline asked.

"Found dead on a ledge of the cliff overlooking Niagara Falls, is what I read online. Though not in a barrel," Nona added. "Sometimes the clues are the details that are not present." She grinned.

"What is the motive to kill him?" Pauline asked, unsure about this woman's humor, or if she really thought that was a clue.

"Well, there is also the crane the police brought in to lift the body from the cliff," she said, her brow furrowed in concentration. "I was surprised at how fast they set the crane up."

"It was almost like they knew it had happened before the police were called," Pauline puzzled. The server arrived just then with their meals.

"You know, Pauline, I think you are onto something there. They only held us for questioning for thirty minutes. How could they have had the entire crime scene set up and cordoned off, crane and all, in such a short time?"

"Seems unlikely to me," Pauline agreed. "Was that the chef's wife, standing with the detective when we left?"

Nona pulled out her cellular phone and entered a Google search for the chef, which brought up pictures of him, and his wife. She turned the phone towards Pauline and Pauline nodded her head in confirmation. "It does look like her."

The two ate in companionable silence until Pauline finished her chicken, wiped her mouth and said, "How was his wife already on scene, in just minutes, unless she knew something was going to happen?"

"I guess that rules out the loudmouth. It had to be the wife!" Nona said and tossed her napkin on her plate.

"May I take your plate, miss?" the slender server asked, appraising their empty plates. "I hope your meal was to your satisfaction?"

Pauline nodded. "Yes, it was extraordinary. Would you get the chef so we can thank him personally?"

"Unfortunately, the head chef called in sick today. The sous chef who has made your meal is very busy right now, as you can imagine. Though, if you think it is extraordinary today, you must come back for it again when Executive Chef Pierre is cooking— this dish is his speciality."

The two women murmured additional thanks, and the server left them to the pressing matter of suspects.

"We have a couple of good suspects," Pauline said. "The loudmouth and the wife. We need to get back to the crime scene and bully that detective into giving us the dirt on both of them."

Nona pinched her lips and then said, "I don't know about the wife. Do you know that the name of the infamous Poulet a la Bonne Femme dish translated means *chicken of the good wife*? Could be something to that." She shrugged. "Besides, you said the detective wouldn't share."

"That is why we have to bully him," Pauline said. "Old ladies can lean on people without them getting upset. We are the superheroes others only dream of being."

"Are you sure about that?"

THEY TWO WOMEN rode in a taxi back to the Falls, where the crime scene was taped off and lit by industrial lamps. Detective Smith was talking to a group of what looked like news reporters and appeared harassed. He welcomed their arrival by striding over to greet the two women, escaping the reporters under the guise of having witnesses to interview.

He led them inside a portable command post, which was only a garden-variety shed, brought to the scene for a makeshift office. When the three were inside and the door shut, he said, "You saved me back there. Those reporters were never going away. Now, what can I do for you?"

"Tell us about the loudmouth and the wife," Nona demanded.

He laughed. "I can't share information about witnesses with the public."

"We could leave, and on our way out, set the rat pack back on you," Pauline threatened. "You know me. I am not just any old witness."

"Okay," he said, grinning, "but I want something good from you in exchange."

"We think it's the loudmouth, or the wife," Nona said. "We're only going by what we've seen. You, however, may know more."

"Then I'm sorry to disappoint you, ladies," Smith said. "Both of them have solid alibis. In fact, you're part of the loudmouth's alibi. The chef was killed while you were waiting in the kitchen."

"Then why did he want to leave so desperately?" Pauline asked.

Smith smirked wryly. "Because he has some outstanding legal issues that he preferred not to discuss with the police today. He isn't a murderer, though—or not that we know of, anyhow."

"And what about the chef's wife?" Nona asked. "She was on the scene quickly, it seemed to us."

"She and her husband, the deceased, live just around the corner," Smith said. "She came to see what the commotion was, not knowing it was her husband's body being found."

"That is what she says," Pauline said. "But what was she doing before she heard the commotion?"

"Again, a solid alibi, I'm afraid," Smith said. "She was having her hair done, and the salon has confirmed that. It was as she was arriving back home that she saw the crowd at the top of the Falls and went to look."

"Hmm," Pauline said. "That seems to rule out our favorite suspects. Who do you suspect?"

"I haven't got a suspect," Smith said. "Based on the initial reports, I'm writing this up as suicide."

"Why would he kill himself?" Nona cried. "Did he leave a note?"

"We haven't found a note," Smith said, "but that proves nothing. As to why? His wife says he was depressed that he hadn't received the recognition he deserved. Felt his best years were slipping away with no growth in his career. You can probably remember days like that when you were younger."

"So much for the *good* wife theory," Nona grumbled under her breath.

"It will not do, Detective," Pauline said. "He was about to give a class to thirty admiring students."

Smith laughed. "That's probably what pushed him over the edge, if you'll pardon the pun. A world-class chef giving cooking lessons to tourists. Not exactly the pinnacle of anyone's career, is it?"

"I read in The Inquirer he was about to land an American

TV deal. That doesn't sound like someone on the brink of suicide to me!" Nona scoffed.

Pauline and Nona looked at each other. They knew they were right, and it was just a matter of proving it.

"Perhaps you are being a little hasty," Pauline said.

He shrugged. "This case is a wrap, and there's not much left to do beyond the paperwork. So, unless you have something that absolutely and irrefutably overthrows my conclusion, I'll bid you goodnight."

The two women walked slowly away from the scene, mingling with the visitors who were admiring the brightly lit falls. They stopped in front of a vintage placard showing a woman going over the Falls in a barrel.

"Wait," Nona said, excitedly pointing to the placard. "It's not about the clues we have deduced already. It is about what's missing. See, I told you."

"What is missing? You are not going to start with the barrel cliché again, are you?" Pauline waved her hand in dismissal of the placard.

"No, no. But it gave me inspiration," Nona said, waggling her eyebrows. "It's not what's missing, rather *who's missing*! The hotel chef, Chef Pierre. The server said he was not at work and that this chicken dish was *his speciality*. Correct me if I am wrong, but that means he's an expert who has devoted significant time and effort to perfecting this dish."

Pauline's eyes widened. "Aha. I see. And the tabloids say the celebrity chef was about to land a television deal because of that exact dish. I think you have a winning theory here. Now we need a plan to unmask him for the murderer he is."

BACK AT THE HOTEL, the two sleuths set to work at the bank of public computers in the business suite. Within an hour, they had all the information they needed, as well as a plan.

"Okay. Here's the plan," Nona said. "I will call the chef at home. When he answers, I will pretend to be the American television company and invite him to prepare the chicken dish for me at his restaurant here in the hotel tomorrow afternoon."

"Good. At the same time, I will contact the young detective and let him know of our trap, and he and I will also dine in the restaurant for lunch," Pauline confirmed.

"And you can watch the rest of the plan unfold with the detective." Nona beamed with pride that she had come up with the plan.

"The detective will witness the murderer's confession!"

"And there won't be much to do . . . beyond more paperwork," Nona mocked the young detective's arrogance.

THE NEXT AFTERNOON, the plan was in place, and the trap to catch this Michelin man was set.

Nona sat at an oversized table in the middle of the hotel's bustling lunch crowd, while Pauline and Detective Smith sat at a nearby table for two.

Under the pretense of being an American television headhunter, Nona explained to the server that she was there to conduct a meeting with Chef Pierre. Within ten minutes, Chef Pierre arrived table-side to deliver his Poulet Bonne Femme.

Miss Riddell and Detective Smith watched as the chef took a seat at Nona's table. Even if she hadn't been able to read lips, Pauline could hear the conversation clearly from her seat.

"You know, Chef, this dish was delicious, however, how can

you claim it to be *your* speciality, when in fact you stole it from Chef Corsair at the Niagara Falls Vineyard?"

"You blasted tourists. You think you can learn to cook like the famous Chef Pierre. In a day, no less. I think not . . . and I careened that pirate. There will be no planks in his future. I was the one robbed of my recipe, and I have put an end to that poacher!"

"Bork bork bork," Nona snickered like the famous puppet chef.

"Sounds like a confession to me," Pauline said to Smith, who was standing beside her watching. He was quick to act.

The chef continued his barrage while being handcuffed. Pierre was bleating a string of expletives at Nona and all of the restaurant patrons as he caused a ruckus all the way through the lobby and out the front door.

"Job well done, Pauline." Nona put her hand out for a high five.

Meeting her new friend's hand in the air, Pauline agreed. "We make an excellent team!"

"I AM glad we decided to get the chicken one more time before leaving," Nona said the following day as they had lunch together.

"Although I will not eat this dish again anytime soon—twice in one long weekend is enough for me," Pauline said, looking up from her newspaper.

"This was a hoot. We should do this again sometime."

"Maybe without the murder," Pauline replied.

"Eh, what's the fun in that?" Nona said, laughing. "How about a craft fair, in the desert? I know a travel agency that can get us a good deal." Nona grinned. "By the way, do you quilt?"

"Look at this, Nona." Pauline folded the newspaper open and pushed it across the table to her companion.

"Says here the wife is going to sue Chef Pierre for the rights to the recipe, and that she and the owner of the vineyard are going to contract for the celebrity chef television series."

"Maybe there was something to the wife theory after all?" Pauline smirked.

RECIPE POULET-BONNE-FEMME
Ingredients (serves 4):

- 1 pound of boneless chicken
- 8–12 small red potatoes - halved
- 1/2 pound bacon cut into 1/2" portions
- 1 yellow onion - sliced
- 1 cup of mushrooms - sliced
- 1 bunch green onions - chopped
- 2 Tbsp parsley
- 1 tsp thyme
- Salt and pepper

Preparation:

Fry the bacon until slightly crisp, then remove. Season chicken and fry in bacon grease until brown. Remove.

Next, brown potato halves in the bacon fat, then remove.

Sauté the yellow onions and mushrooms until lightly browned, then remove.

Layer half of the ingredients in a pot (cast iron if you have one); layer half of the chicken on the bottom, then half of the potatoes, sautéed onions, mushrooms and the bacon.

Season with salt and pepper and thyme.

Repeat the layers.

Place half of the chopped green onions and parsley on top.

Bake, covered for 40 minutes at 350 degrees Fahrenheit. Uncover and finish baking for another 15 minutes.

Remove from the oven and top with the remaining parsley and green onion. Serve.

SASSY SENIOR SLEUTHS MYSTERIES

2

DEADLY DUNES

P.C. JAMES
KATHRYN MYKEL

DEADLY DUNES

Mini Mystery #2

"Does it seem strange that we're the only old ladies on a bus full of twentysomethings?" Nona asked Pauline, who was sitting next to her in the window seat. She had been eyeing the other passengers.

"Yes, something is wrong. Are you sure we boarded the right coach?" Pauline eyed her friend.

"Why are you looking at me like that? I wasn't in charge of 'make sure we get on the right bus today.'" She frowned. "Was I?"

"It's unlikely that these young men are on a tour of the Navajo Crafts Fair. And not with all that gear."

"They sure have a lot of gear . . ." Nona pointed to the overflowing bag of goggles, gloves, and helmets. "Oh goodness, please don't tell me we are going to a motorcycle race? That would be dreadful!"

The occasional cactus and Joshua tree were the only forms of life they had seen in over an hour. "In the desert?" Pauline shook her head. "No."

They sat in silent disbelief until Nona exclaimed, "That foolish travel agency!" She slapped her hand on the seat in front of her.

"Settle down. I'll go talk to the driver and find out just where this coach is headed," Pauline said as she brushed past Nona to the aisle.

She could've just asked the guy next to us, Nona grumbled under her breath as Pauline walked away.

Pauline returned a minute later. "Well, I have good news and bad news. Which one do you want first?"

"Good news . . . No, the bad news—No . . . Yes, give me the bad news." Nona gripped the back of the seat in front of her and braced herself.

"You are so dramatic," Pauline dismissed. "As we suspected, we are NOT going to the Crafts Fair."

"Ohhhkay, what is the good news?" Nona shifted to the edge of the seat.

"Well, the good news is subjective . . ." Pauline paused.

"And . . ." Nona wiggled in her seat.

"We are going to be the first seventy-year-old women to compete in their dune buggy derby," Pauline said.

"Say what?"

"A dune buggy derby. You have heard of dune buggies, I'm sure," Pauline said.

"Of course I have, but we didn't sign up for that." Nona wrinkled her face again.

"That's what I said," Pauline answered, "but the bus driver said, and I quote, *Ah, no problem, ladies, we'll get you sorted—they'll have extra gear and padding for you. Who knows, you might even have fun!*"

"Well, we will have fun. We're spry, Pauline. Fit as a fiddle," Nona said and slapped the back of the seat again. "You still run, don't you?"

"Only when chased!" Pauline smirked. "I am not sure what to expect, in terms of what 'accommodations' they will have for two *distinguished* women."

"Who are you calling distinguished?" Nona guffawed. "We had better use the loo before we get off the bus, then!"

AN HOUR LATER, Nona grinned and said, "There's no turning back now." She spun to look over at her friend through floppy goggles, and pulled on the chinstrap of her oversized helmet.

Harnessed in tight sitting next to her, Pauline had a white-knuckle grip on the 'oh no' bar in front of her. "I do not know whose idea it was to let you drive."

"What . . .? I still have a valid driver's license! I am old. Not dead." Nona chortled.

"Well, let us hope we make it through this in one piece," Pauline yelled over the blare of the starting horn, and their buggy rumbled to life.

"Hold on, I want to find out what this thing has under the hood!" Nona grinned and slammed her foot down on the accelerator. The two women flung back against the seat with a rush as the buggy took off, and then the wind and gravity forced them back again as the buggy charged up the first dune.

"Don't let off the gas!" Pauline yelled, alarmed that her derriere was no longer connected to the seat as they raced their way back down the other side of the dune.

They looked at each other in horror as a double thud shuddered underneath them.

"What was that?" they yelled at the same time.

"Pull over!" Pauline yelled and pointed to the right.

"Pull over? This isn't the highway." Nona laughed as she let off the accelerator and the buggy came to a stop on a flat section of desert sand.

They unbuckled their helmets and helped each other with the harnesses. "Darn it, we were in the lead," Nona said as the wind whipped her hair across her face and the buggy behind them raced by.

"What is that?" Nona stared down the dune at what had made the thudding noise.

As they got close to the long dark object in the sand, Pauline quickened her pace. "It looks like a dumped carpet someone wanted to be rid of."

"They must not have dug the hole deep enough." Nona joked and then peered closer. Two feet stuck out of one end—it was a body, rolled up in a rather expensive-looking oriental rug. And they had just run it over!

"Now I'm going to pull back the carpet and see if we recognize the person," Nona said.

Pauline raised her hand to stop Nona. "We can't touch anything. The police will need to examine it as we found it."

"Well, they can't," Nona replied. "We hit it with the buggy. I'd say it's been disturbed."

"How could we know the body?" Pauline asked. "We're in the middle of a desert. We don't live near here, and besides, the body could have been here for years."

Nona pulled at one corner of the carpet. From what she could see, it was a young woman, blonde haired, with a freckled face.

"She's very young," Nona said. "Twenties."

Pauline gasped and said, "We saw her in the hotel dining room last evening."

"You're right, but how is that possible? What are the chances?"

Pauline said, "You have one of those mobile phones. Call the authorities and the event organizers. We need to hand this over to them."

"I'll never get a signal here," Nona said. "We're a hundred miles from Vegas."

"But not miles from that over there," Pauline said, pointing behind Nona to the unlikely subdivision in the middle of the desert.

Nona called, and soon the authorities were on their way.

While waiting for the authorities, Nona and Pauline continued to speculate. "It's a message to someone. The girl was meant to be found, though I imagine not by us."

"What message? 'Blondie sleeps with the carpet'?" Nona said with air quotes.

"Who would have been in the lead today, if we hadn't shown up and you hadn't been outdoing the men in the 'Little Old Lady from Pasadena' buggy?"

"There were two teams trading insults on the bus," Nona said. "Each claiming they'd win today."

"Leave the other in the dust, to be exact," Pauline said. "They must know this girl. It is a possibility that she's the girlfriend of one team member, and the other team killed her for some indiscretion or other."

"Some indiscretion?" Nona questioned.

"You know what I mean," Pauline said. "This is a message that another team would uncover, but we beat them to it."

Nona nodded. "Seems simple enough. We will wrap the case up before the police even get here."

THE POLICE WERE quick to follow up on Pauline's theory and question the two rival teams. However, neither team claimed to recognize the girl at all, nor did any of the other team's members. There wasn't anything more to be done with no actual evidence. The police collected names and contacts and advised everyone to stay put in Las Vegas until cleared.

"That is disappointing," Pauline said. "I was sure I was onto it. I cannot imagine any other explanation. Only someone who had knowledge about the course would have known where to half bury the body. The race must have something to do with it."

Minutes later, Nona grinned. "Aha, I've got it." She started pacing.

"Well, tell me?" Pauline eyed her with suspicion.

Nona began listing off the theories with her fingers. "One, we're just outside Las Vegas."

"And?"

"I am getting to it. It's classic." Nona paused for dramatic effect and nodded her head in affirmation. "Hostage situation . . . gone wrong!" She curtseyed. "Ouch. I'm sore." She rubbed her backside.

Pauline tried to make sense of it. "What makes you think that?"

"Well, because everything is about money here!"

"That seems like a big leap, but it is a theory. We will need some proof," Pauline said doubtfully. "Especially since we were not . . . exactly 'on point' with the first theory.

"Wait, wait, wait, hold up . . . Two . . ." Nona said, raising a second finger.

"Okay. What else?" Pauline asked as they walked back to the bus.

"Two . . . Alien abduction."

Pauline shook her head at the absurdity.

"Did you notice the A51 buggy?" Nona began laughing. "Ha, okay, actually that's all I've got."

Pauline said, "So we can safely say we are going to investigate option one now."

Nona handed her racing gear to the bus driver and the two friends got back on the bus. "This sure was an exciting day. I am bushed."

"It certainly wasn't a crafts fair! We can get some shut-eye, as we have a couple hours' ride back to the hotel."

"Sure, but I'll sleep with one eye open." She squinted one eye and bulged the other at Pauline. "We might be on a bus with a murderer."

THE HOTEL WAS BUSTLING as the two seniors headed for the elevator.

"Are you packing heat tonight?" Nona asked, theatrically scanning the lobby, stopping at the boutique, and admiring the gorgeous fashion scarves that hung on racks just inside. She urged Pauline over to the window with half a dozen mannequins sporting fringe haircuts.

"I'm not 'packing heat,'" Pauline said, laughing. "Aren't you the one with the mob connections?" Her eyes followed Nona's to the mannequins, and she grimaced. Fashion wasn't one of Pauline's interests. "Maybe you should cut your hair short like that, Nona," Pauline teased.

"Are you kidding? I could definitely pull that off, no problem. Why do you think I have mob connections?" Nona patted her hair. "More like CIA connections. I would like one of these gorgeous vintage sterling silver fashion combs."

The two women meandered through the lobby past reception and the overworked slot machines towards the elevator. At each of the machines sat an elderly player, staring hopefully at the flashing screen.

"Look at this." Pauline pulled a flier off the elevator wall, stuffed it in Nona's hand and said, "Freckles."

"Yes, that's the girl . . . She had freckles." Nona squinted to get a better look. "Oh, her name is Freckles?"

"No. Put your glasses on and check again."

Nona pulled her reading glasses down from her head to her nose. "Oh, the horse's name is Freckles! The girl was its rider."

Pauline nodded as she pushed the button for the penthouse. "I am amazed that you got us into the penthouse suite."

"Well, technically, it's the staff quarters *for* the penthouse suite, but you'd never know it!" Nona shrugged and flashed a coy smile as she continued reading the flier. "It says here she's an Olympic-champion horse dancer."

"I believe they call it dressage," Pauline confirmed. "And I suspect we have solved the case!"

"Yes, and I know just what you're thinking." Nona pointed. "Animal rights activists killed the girl!"

"Well, that is not exactly what I was thinking. I am not sure animal rights activists are that violent," Pauline said, "but somebody was."

"They may not have meant to kill her," Nona speculated, then cocked her head and waggled her eyebrows. "There's still the 'hostage situation gone wrong' theory."

"Then why dump her body where it could be found on the course?" Pauline asked. "After all, whoever did this was incredibly unlucky in burying her in the exact place the racers from the hotel were going to drive over the next day, or they wanted her found."

Nona frowned in concentration. "The horse did it." She

waggled her eyebrows again and flashed Pauline a mischievous grin.

"Okay, now you are just being silly, Nona."

They stepped out of the elevator and made their way down the corridor to their suite.

"All we have done so far is speculate. Let us put the clues together," Pauline suggested.

"Okay, well, we've got Las Vegas, a horse dancer and an oriental rug . . . Sounds like a bad bar joke!"

"We need to find out more about this girl—who her friends were, lovers, manager," Pauline said. "We will do that first thing tomorrow."

"Why not tonight?" Nona asked. "I overheard the racers saying there would be a party in the bar tonight. Some of the show people might be there too."

Pauline nodded. "You're right. So, a shower to shake out some of this dust, and dinner to give us fuel for the evening."

DRESSED FOR SUCCESS, the two sleuths were back in the elevator in less than forty-five minutes. Pauline took two brochures of Freckles and its rider from the hallway, saying, "We can show these to people and ask who saw her last night or before."

The elevator chimed, and the doors opened onto the first floor. "Somewhere here," Pauline said as they exited, her eyes sweeping across the room and taking in the throngs of people at the bar and in the casino, "is someone who killed that girl, and we are going to get them."

Pauline and Nona dined just long enough for a quick one-course meal and then headed for the bar where most of their fellow buggy racers would be celebrating the day.

"They are a callous bunch," Pauline said, frowning at the noise and hilarity. There was quite a party starting as the buggy racers and a group of admiring girls relived the excitement of the race.

"Not those," Nona said, pointing to a quieter, somber group against a far wall.

"You're right," Pauline replied. "Maybe they knew her and are coming to terms with her death."

"Or with their part in it," Nona observed grimly. "Even if they are just a bunch of kids."

"To us, they're kids, but they appear to be of legal age. We should find out if the buggy racers and the show acts are linked," Pauline said. "Or did they just meet and mingle?"

"She was a good-looking girl. They're good-looking guys," Nona said. "We don't need to spend a lot of time on that."

"But what connects them?"

Nona burst out laughing. "You really are a *Miss Riddell*, aren't you? What connects them, indeed?"

Pauline flushed red. "I mean, why was she killed and dumped where 'they' would find her? You are the one who proposed an 'abduction,' so stop giggling and think."

Nona nodded seriously. "Why don't we ask that sorry-looking bunch some hard questions." She crossed the room to stand in front of the four twenty-somethings, who stared back at her in puzzlement.

"Which one of you was with the murdered girl last night?" she demanded.

They glanced at her and at each other from the corner of their eyes. None would face her.

"What makes you think any of us were?" one muttered.

"Because," Pauline said, joining Nona, "everyone else is partying, and you four look like you committed murder."

"Tell us or tell the police," Pauline continued. "If you don't, we will."

They all glanced at each other, silent until one said, "She was with me at dinnertime, okay, but I didn't kill her. I swear." He put his hands up in defense.

"Did you tell the police you were the last one to see her?" Pauline questioned.

He shook his head. "I panicked and said I didn't know her. We'd just been sitting here discussing it and agreed we were going to go to the police and tell them when you two showed up. Who are you, anyway?"

Taking on the bad cop role, Nona said, "Your guardian angels, if you're telling the truth, or your worst nightmare, if you're not."

"Did she tell you anything that might help identify her killer?" Pauline asked.

"We did little talking," he said and dropped his head. This should have sounded like a joke, but no one was laughing.

"The police will not buy this 'I know nothing' story, and I don't either," Pauline said. "What is it?"

"It's . . . It's nothing," one said. "Nothing."

"Then you should have no problem telling us what it is, if it's nothing," Nona said, leaning her fists on the table and glaring at each one of them.

"Something she said," the lover boy replied. "When we were partying, she said she knew something to make us all rich, and she laughed about it hysterically, making a huge scene."

"We were too far gone to take her up on it," another guy said. "But people would have overheard her."

"How many people might have overheard her say this?" Pauline asked.

"Few, ma'am," the lone girl said. She pressed close to the guy who had claimed to be with the murdered girl the night before, as if to comfort him. *He must be quite something*, Pauline thought, *to have girls so eager to be with him.*

Nona and Pauline scowled at the group. "Angel or nightmare? Your choice."

"All right, just us and the creep over there," the girl said. "But don't look." She whipped her head back. "Or he'll know we told you." She peeked out from behind her long straight bangs, and her eyes flicked to a group of party animals behind them, while she slipped her hand around the guy's arm and pulled him closer.

"How do we recognize the creep?" Nona asked.

"Older, forty-ish, tall, greasy black hair, lots of tattoos, real mean-looking." She shrugged. "You can't miss him. He stands out."

"How did he hear and no one else?" Pauline asked, watching their expressions.

"I thought she was with him, at first," the young Casanova said. "She said she wasn't, but he was always just there. Like he was monitoring her."

"And none of you can remember what the scheme was?" Pauline asked. Would the sudden accusation trigger something in them?

They all looked at each other. The girl said, "We were, you know, partying. We hardly knew where we were." She twirled her long straight hair around the fingers of her free hand.

"Are you kids rich or famous?" Nona asked.

"Not yet," the guy said, "but you can make good money racing buggies, so someday we will be. Are you?"

"Are we what?"

"Are you granny detectives or something? Is that why you're asking us all these questions?"

Nona scoffed. "No," she said, and laughed. "Remember, we

had the misfortune of finding the young lady rolled in the carpet."

She continued, "We'll leave you to your thoughts, kids, but if I were you, I'd get to the police before whoever killed the girl decides leaving you above ground is too risky."

Pauline and Nona walked away, skirting the raucous partiers while sizing up 'the creep.'

"What do you think?" Pauline asked as they crossed the lobby, heading for the elevators.

"We should call the police right now because if that guy is *the guy,* he's now seen us talking to those kids and we'll be at risk too.

"We are still no nearer to getting the 'why,'" Pauline said. "The police can tell us how, when, possibly where, but we need to find that 'why.'"

They rode the elevator, stopping at multiple floors, letting passengers on and off. Nona noticed a sign on the fourth floor for a rug sale. "Did you see that?" She pointed to the hallway as the doors closed.

"I did, why?" Pauline asked.

"I'll bet that's where the carpet came from," Nona said. "We have to go back up and check it out."

When the last passengers exited the elevator, they sent it back to the fourth floor and stepped out into a ballroom, set up as a carpet bazaar, designed with a Persian theme. They wandered between the rugs, their eyebrows twitching so high they might bounce off the ceiling, looking at the prices.

"I knew visitors to Vegas were thought to be rich," Pauline said, "but not this rich."

"They are authentic, madam, and the price can't be beat," a voice behind them said.

They turned and froze. It was him. The man the boys had pointed out as the girl's companion the night before.

"I am sure they are," Pauline said, smiling in what she hoped was a disarming fashion. "We are just not wealthy enough for these carpets."

"We have several affordable payment plans that will help with any budget. You can own one of these masterpieces, even on a modest budget. And they aren't just beautiful, they're an investment. This one, for example, is five thousand today, but it will be worth twice that in only a few years' time. I assure you, this is an investment to top up any pension."

"Did you know the murdered girl?" Nona snapped.

His expression darkened. "I did," he said, "and I wish I'd stayed with her that night, but she insisted, and I had no right . . ."

"We were talking to the racers," Pauline said, intending to make their questioning less pointed. "They said much the same thing."

He nodded. "They would," he said. "I suspect them, though I don't understand why they would harm her."

"How did you know her?" Nona asked.

"Brittany came in here when she wasn't practicing on her horse. That was her name you know, though everyone called her Freckles because that was her horse's name. We talked, and I thought we had become friendly." He paused. "I see now the girl just wanted to have fun."

"The boys said she told them she knew a secret that would make them all rich," Nona persisted. "Do you know what she meant by that?"

His expression grew even darker. "They said that, did they? I hope they told the police?"

"They hadn't . . ." Nona began, stopping when Pauline elbowed her.

"I am sure they have by now," Pauline said.

"Foolish kids," he said. "They care for nothing but drinking and racing." His words sounded harmless enough, but his expression said anything but.

"We must go," Nona said, "but we'll come again when we have more time." She ran out of the room, with Pauline trying to make their departure less rude with thanks and smiling leave-taking. She caught up with Nona at the elevator.

"What was that about?" Pauline asked.

"We must find that detective and tell him," Nona said. "If the kids sit there drinking all night and never call the police, some-thing bad might happen to *them* too."

The elevator took them to the ground floor, where they asked the woman at reception to call the police detective for them.

"There's no need, ma'am," the receptionist said. "He's here interviewing the other acts."

They confronted the detective as he was leaving a room set aside for interviews, and Nona launched into a jumbled tale of carpets, sinister salesmen, secrets, and threats to the life of the racers.

"Whoa there, ma'am, do you have any evidence?" the detec-tive questioned.

Pauline explained more precisely what they had surmised.

The detective nodded. "Look, ladies. I know you had a shock this morning, and you gave us an excellent theory about those kids. I'm not saying you didn't, but you have to leave this vigi-lante stuff behind and get some rest. All this will be less fright-ening after a good night's sleep."

"How can I get a good night's sleep knowing there is a murderer with access to fancy carpets stalking the hotel only three floors below us, and who now knows, that we know, the girl was going to inform on him?"

The detective's expression grew stony. "First, we know Mr. Persaude—the carpet salesman, as you call him—very well. He's an important proprietor. Has been for years now. You may not like his tattoos, but that doesn't make him a killer. Leave this to us. We'll catch the girl's killer soon enough and with the evidence to make it stick."

"Detective," Pauline asked, hoping to save the situation, which was sinking like an iceberg had hit it. "How did she die?"

He frowned. "I guess it's all right to tell you. You'll hear it on the news soon enough. Someone stabbed her with a weapon shaped like an ice pick."

"Stick 'em with the pointy end," Nona mumbled under her breath.

"So anyone could have done it," Pauline said. "It would not take much force to puncture a body with that."

"Not much," the detective said, "but it still takes a cool customer to do something like that—stab someone while looking them in the eye, I mean."

"Or someone who's hardened to it," Nona said.

"If you're still thinking Mr. Persaude, you're wrong. You may think he looks like a criminal but he's not."

"Come on, Nona," Pauline said, dragging her away.

Nostrils flaring, Nona said, "I don't care how long Persaude's been an entrepreneur in a town like this or how much money he launders through fake charities. I don't trust him one bit."

"Maybe, but the detective is right," Pauline said. "We need rest to clear our heads and stop us running off on tangents."

"Your room has two beds," Nona said. "I vote we bunk together until we catch the killer."

"I agree," Pauline said. "Now, let us grab your stuff and get some sleep. We got this one wrong twice now, and we cannot get a third one wrong or the detective will lock *us* up."

PAULINE LAY IN BED, staring at the ceiling in the darkness. The flashing lights out on the Strip were flickering on the stucco ceiling, leaving short-lived shadows among the garish colors. *That boy, the one who was with the girl they called Freckles, had to have known what the plan was. Did he kill her so he wouldn't have to share the loot? He didn't look the type. The creep did, but he seemed more like the girl's protector. So why would he kill her? Is there something or someone we missed?*

It was a long time before sleep overtook Pauline. Her sleep was restless and filled with dreams of smirking boys and men with tattoos, armed with thin shiny blades that flickered and glinted in the pulsing lights. She woke to find Nona sitting on the end of her bed in deep contemplation.

"Have you solved it?" Pauline asked.

"I can't get that creep out of my mind," Nona said. "The kids didn't like him, and I don't either."

"The Casanova guy must have known what the secret was if he was with the girl," Pauline said. "Even if the others didn't hear what she said."

"You think it was him?"

"I don't know," Pauline said. "Something isn't right."

"Murder's what's not right," Nona retorted.

"Obviously, but that is not it," Pauline said. "We need to bring those kids and the creep together with the police detective, like they do in the old crime shows, and talk until someone makes a mistake."

"They'd never go along with it," Nona said. "Why should they? What happens in Vegas . . ."

"Because we're going to announce who did it, and why," Pauline said.

Nona eyed her friend with speculation. "We're going to do that, are we?"

"It is do or die, Nona. Are you up for it?"

"So serious, Miss Riddell. Yes, of course you know I am!" She clapped her hands and giggled.

IT TOOK some persuading to convince the detective this wasn't a crazy scheme, but he admitted having them together and putting them under pressure may force the breakthrough he needed.

"It's your show, Miss Riddell," Nona said, happy to step back and watch how things panned out.

Following the method used by so many great fictional detectives, Pauline laid out the circumstantial evidence against the creep, whose angry rebuttals made him seem even more the guilty party.

Then she walked the group through how the young buggy racer could have done it and placed the body in the course, so it appeared he was framed. Who would imagine a murderer would expose his victim like this? And all to keep the money the girl had told him she knew how to get. By the time Pauline was finished, he was white as a ghost and could only stammer "I didn't do it" in a way that convinced no one.

The girl, who was still clutching him, however, was rigid with fury. She jumped to her feet, spilling her purse to the ground. Pauline saw what she'd been hoping to see.

"Detective," Pauline said, "that comb. Look at the handle."

The girl grabbed the fashion comb and thrust its silver handle under the buggy driver's chin.

"Keep back," she said, her voice now cold and even. "We're leaving, and no one better try to stop me!"

The group watched the two step backwards to the door. The girl's eyes were pinpointed on Pauline and the detective. She didn't see the buggy driver's hand come up from nowhere to grab her wrist. In one move, he twisted away, and turned her arm back, and she dropped the comb.

The police converged and handcuffed her.

"DID YOU KNOW IT WAS HER?" the detective asked Pauline. "Or was that just dumb luck?"

"She was too eager to answer our questions," Pauline said, "and it made me uneasy, though I didn't know why."

"And when did you know?"

"I had some pretty vivid dreams last night," Pauline said. "My mind was wrestling with all the clues. I went over our meeting with them and replayed all the conversations."

"Well, she spilled it all," the detective said to Nona and Pauline. "She saw him and Freckles—I mean 'Brittany,' that is the victim's name. She saw how much he wanted Brittany. So she stole one of the Persian rugs to make it look like the merchant was the killer. She texted Brittany from the guy's phone and lured her into a trap in the parking lot. The girl deleted the texts, but we'll be able to trace the records. She stabbed her with the end of her comb, bundled the body in her car, wrapped it in the rug, of course, and buried it where she knew lover boy would find it. The perfect case for revenge of a woman slighted."

"But you didn't know she had that comb," Nona said to Pauline.

"I deduced it when we got off the elevator to go to the interrogation room." Pauline pointed to the hair salon across the lobby, where hair accessories were on display, including some wicked-looking combs with long cylindrical handles.

"What is it?" Nona asked, stretching her neck to see what Pauline was pointing at.

"The shiny silver hair combs you were looking at . . . slim and pointed . . ." Pauline stated.

"Distracted by something shiny! Now, that's funny, but I'm still disappointed." Nona frowned. "No mobsters, activists or aliens . . . Just a jealous spat over a dull boy."

"Love makes even dull people desirable, Nona," Pauline said primly, feeling she'd evened the score for Nona's '*Miss*' comment earlier. "Even an old spinster like me knows that."

SASSY SENIOR SLEUTHS MYSTERIES

3

THE MAN IN SEAT 13B

P.C. JAMES

KATHRYN MYKEL

THE MAN IN SEAT 13B

Mini Mystery #3

"Nona," Pauline said, when they'd settled themselves in their seats on the tour bus. "What do you think that young man at the back is doing on this excursion?"

Nona looked around as though surveying the passengers, but keeping her focus on the young man Pauline had mentioned. They'd thought his presence odd when they climbed aboard and sat a few seats in front of him. "It is strange," she said. "This isn't the kind of tour that would appeal to a lone young man."

Pauline nodded. "A plantation house and gardens followed by a museum is exactly the opposite of what would appeal, I would think."

There were too few people on the coach for their conversation to be overheard. Still, they said no more on the subject as the coach wended its way through the narrow streets of the island's old capital city and then out into the country.

The coach drew into a driveway lined with palm trees and stopped outside the door of the Eighteenth-Century Great House. Responding to their guide's request to join her outside, Pauline and Nona left the coach and waited with the others.

"He hasn't come out," Nona whispered.

Pauline nodded. "Perhaps it's the museum he wants to see," she said.

AN HOUR LATER, when they returned from the garden tour, the man was still in his seat.

"This isn't right," Pauline said. "He's not right. Let's make his acquaintance, shall we?"

They moved down the bus to the last row, which the man had to himself.

They didn't need to speak to him to know—*he was dead*. A still-wet red stain on his T-shirt told them so. He sat in the window seat with his head slumped back, a straw hat covering his face and his arms folded in his lap.

ANNOYED BY A CHIRPING BEHIND HER, Nona waited impatiently in her seat as Pauline explained *the dead guy in seat 13B* to the bus driver.

"What is he going to do about it?" she asked when Pauline had settled back into the seat next to her.

"He said, 'We'll drop him off at the next stop.'"

"So, we're going to ride around with a dead guy until the next stop . . . at the museum?" Nona shrilled as the bus pulled out onto the country road.

"I questioned the validity of it and he just said, 'Trust me. I handle it.'" Pauline grinned and Nona knew exactly what her friend was thinking. "I guess it is up to us to investigate." They nodded to each other in unison.

"What about the other passengers? Should they be told?" Nona asked.

On top of the chirping, Nona swatted at a fly buzzing around the two septuagenarians. She was going to have a few words with the travel agent at Destinations about the less than ideal conditions during this tour.

Thinking about the dead man's possessions and the chirping, Nona set her handwork quilting project down on the seat and patted Pauline on the knee. She stood up with a gleam in her eye and said, "You stay here. I've got this one!"

In one swift motion, much too fast for a seventy-year-old woman, Nona grabbed one of the bags at the dead man's feet and tossed it on the seat next to him. The contents shifted awkwardly. As she unzipped it, a fat fluffy green parrot let out an ear-piercing squawk and flew straight at her. She dodged left as the parrot flapped by her and made its landing on an empty seat across the aisle.

This time she went to speak to the bus driver to explain *the dead guy in seat 13B . . . and his smuggled parrot,* but she was met with the same response Pauline had been given: 'Trust me. I'll handle it.' Nona wasn't sure what kind of logic was at play here, but the last thing she was going to do was trust a guy who says 'trust me.' She thought everyone knew the code. *Those are the guys you don't trust!*

AT THE MUSEUM, a detective and a uniformed police officer boarded the coach, spoke briefly with the bus driver and then made their way down the bus, questioning the passengers row by row, and searching their bags for weapons. The detective began questioning Pauline and Nona—he was sharp and had taken command of the scene, whereas the island officer was *the muscle.*

"He is a parrot smuggler. We learned about rare green parrots on our excursion yesterday," Nona said and let out an exaggerated sneeze. "Check his other bags."

"Pretty Jewel," the bird squawked behind them, and all three of them turned to see the parrot content on the seat, preening its plumage.

"The bird's name must be Jewel," the officer mumbled.

The detective dismissed Nona's theory. "No, no. Listen, ma'am. He's no parrot smuggler. He's a local performer who puts on performances with his pet parrots. He has the necessary permits, I assure you."

Once all passengers had given their statements and the detective was convinced there were no weapons on their persons, they disembarked for the museum. The officer handed Nona two business cards. "Pretty Jewel," the bird continued as Nona sneezed again.

Pauline and Nona hustled off the coach, and the detective and officer stayed aboard with the bus driver.

"Son of a gun, I thought I was onto something there!" Nona said, while trying to catch up to the other passengers already entering the museum. "I was sure of it," Nona grumbled, entering the museum.

ON ANY OTHER DAY, Pauline might have found the museum's pre-Columbian art and artifacts interesting. Today, the dead body in the coach claimed all her attention. She looked at each exhibit seeing nothing except for the dead man, the bloodstained T-shirt, the parrot, and his bags. She frowned. *Why was he even on this bus tour if he was a local entertainer?* Either the guide or the bus driver let him on, or they both did. *Was this about drugs? Was he a courier? Why all the black duffle bags?*

If he was a courier, he might have been handing the drugs off to a passenger from the ship who was with us on this excursion. Her mind flicked through each passenger on the bus, trying to decide who was the most likely person to be a smuggler. They were all elderly people, mainly women traveling together as she and Nona were. *Who among them might supplement her pension with some illicit drug selling?* It seemed unlikely, and yet the man had been killed.

"Maybe it was a disappointed fan or one of those animal rights groups?" Nona said, as she found Pauline studying old photos of sand at a dig site. "I can't concentrate. I need to know what happened. If people are going to keep dropping every time we go on an adventure, solving the case seems the least we can ask for." Nona stared at Pauline with a straight face.

Ignoring Nona's theatrics, as she had learned to do over the course of their brief friendship, Pauline whispered, "Nona, I think the next logical assumption would be drugs?"

"We should have searched the dead man's bags before the police got on board," Nona said, nodding.

"I think we still have a chance to solve this," Pauline whispered. The museum was as silent as the grave. "Think about it— whoever killed him will have the drugs *on* them."

"Riiight . . . because the detective said he was going to search the bus after all the passengers got off it." Nona put her finger to her lip. "But who?"

"Precisely. Which of our fellow passengers will it be?" Pauline puzzled. "Let's make a list."

"I was so focused on the dead guy, I can hardly remember the few passengers, let alone where they were sitting!" Nona complained. "Even if we figure it out, how are we going to unmask the culprit? It's not like we can strip-search them," Nona said, "and you can be sure the drugs aren't hidden somewhere a casual search would find."

"A trap, we need to set a trap," Pauline replied. "I know just the thing. We need one of those drug-sniffing dogs. Only, where to find one on an island?"

Nona's face lit up in a smile. "Aha, which is why they're doing it *this* way. I think you have it, Pauline."

Pauline nodded. "Yes, there are usually dogs at airports and seaports but not where the cruise ships dock. I have never seen them there."

"Now, all we have to do is tell the police to have a drug-sniffing dog at the gate when our bus returns to the ship, and it's done." Nona opened her bag. "I have their business cards here somewhere. Here's one!" she cried out triumphantly, handing it to Pauline and letting out a big sneeze. "You call. You solved it."

"What are you allergic to?" Pauline asked, shoving a hand-kerchief in Nona's direction.

"I don't know, I can't help it."

Pauline called the number on the card and after some initial reluctance on the police officer's part, arranged for the drug-sniffing dog.

As they disembarked from the coach, Pauline and Nona exchanged knowing grins. A police officer and German shepherd dog were strategically placed at the entrance to the cruise ship dock.

They allowed the rest of the tour's passengers to get ahead of them and watched as one by one each passed the dog without the dog showing a stitch of interest in any of them.

"Oh," Pauline said, deflated. "I was so sure."

Nona nodded sympathetically. "And it was a sensible solution. Just not the right one. Well, we gave it our best shot. The cops will have to solve it without our help."

Pauline nodded. "Though," she said, "there is the Museum After Dark tour later tonight. It might offer one last chance?"

"The driver said he was picking up passengers for that tour also," Nona said. "But we don't know if the guide is the same, and it's doubtful any of the passengers from this afternoon's tour will be on the evening tour."

"I know," Pauline said, "but I think we have sort of eliminated the passengers. For me, now, it is between the driver and the guide."

"But does it have to be a 'thing'?" Nona said. "If the entertainer and the two suspects are all locals, it could have just been a quarrel, maybe over something we know nothing about."

"I don't think he would have been on the bus if it was something of that kind," Pauline said.

"So, we do the night tour?"

"We have to," Pauline replied. "It's our only chance."

"So, what's the plan? I do love the hunt!" Nona said to Pauline, thirty minutes later, as they waited in line for the coach to pick them up again.

"Well, we can check the bus on the off chance the bags are stashed on board somewhere," Pauline replied.

"Doubtful." Nona frowned.

"Okay, we should split up. I'll take the guide and you take the driver," Pauline suggested.

"I always get the smelly ones," Nona grumbled.

"Ladies."

At the greeting, Nona and Pauline both looked up towards the familiar voice. To their surprise, it was the officer and detective from earlier who greeted them as they made their way onto the bus for the second time that day.

"The officer is in plain clothes . . ." Nona sneezed. "Undercover?" She whispered her question to Pauline as they made their way to the back of the coach, abandoning the initial plan.

"They must be in on it," Pauline deduced and handed Nona a fresh handkerchief.

"But we still don't know what 'it' is. I say we lie low until we get into the museum. If he's in on it, he's probably on to *us* too!" Nona blew her nose. "I'll keep this one," she said, holding up the hankie.

The two sleuths made their way in, blending into the middle of the pack of passengers. Inside, they had the perfect vantage point, huddled around a grouping of ancient relics on pedestal displays near the security detectors. Their position was strategic, so they would have a quick escape if things went sideways. The two women watched the police officer work the crowd with a mischievous twinkle in his eye.

"The detective is nowhere to be seen," Nona said, swiveling her head around, looking for him.

"He's up to something," Pauline said. "Oh, don't look, he's coming this way."

"Is that the bus driver, too?" Nona asked and then turned to

Pauline, red faced and with bulging eyes. "and what's in the cop's pocket?"

"Quick, do something," Pauline snapped.

The museum's alarms blared obnoxiously overhead. The crowd of museum patrons began murmuring and pointing. All eyes were on Nona, who was standing there with the ancient pre-Columbian relic in her hand.

"Well, that was something," Pauline yelled with her hands behind her back.

From out of nowhere, the detective said, "Ladies, are you trying to steal this from the museum?" He plucked the ornate statue out of Nona's hand and passed it to the approaching security guard.

The plainclothes officer and bus driver flanked Nona on both sides. "You're going to have to come with me, ma'am" the officer said, grabbing her arm and ushering Nona towards the security detectors at the main entrance, followed by the bus driver, the detective and Pauline.

Just as the overhead alarm subsided, another volley of alarms rang out from behind them. Nona stopped and turned. Pauline stood behind them all with one of the ancient statues in *her* hands. She smiled and shrugged.

With his attention now diverted to Pauline, Nona grabbed at the police officer's pocket and pulled out a large black velvet bag. She emptied the bag into her hand and hundreds of brilliant uncut diamonds cascaded over her palm and onto the floor. "It's them!" she pointed and shouted. "They killed the man on the bus, and he's a diamond smuggler!" she said triumphantly, holding her hand out as proof.

"Well done!" Pauline cheered.

"IT WAS JUST A DIVERSION," Nona explained to the museum's security guards. "We had to do something to catch them before they left the museum . . . or worse." She raised her eyebrows and shrugged one of her shoulders. "I've seen it done on TV, but I couldn't know for sure if there would actually be alarms under the statues."

It took a while to convince the guards that they weren't really trying to steal priceless relics from the museum. But when they were satisfied, the ladies recounted the tale of the dead man in seat 13B. The detective backed up their suspicions. "Job well done, ladies. I have been investigating the bus driver and the officer, but I haven't been able to catch them in the act. I guess I needed a woman's eye," he teased, and Nona's face reddened again.

Pauline explained, "It finally started coming together for *me* when Nona said the driver was smelly and then she sneezed when we walked by the police officer.

"First, she sneezed when the police officer was on the bus earlier in the day dealing with the dead man. I thought it might have been the bird, but then she sneezed again when she handed me the police officer's business card. Coincidence maybe, but then she sneezed once more when we got back on the bus for the night tour."

"The cop is wearing the same cheap cologne," Nona said in between sneezes.

Pauline continued explaining, "We knew the driver had to be in on it because the dead man was on the tour. And he was the only one who was not frisked when you came on board to investigate. That was confirmed when we spotted the driver with the police officer inside the museum."

"I suspect you'll find the driver shot his accomplice, the man on the bus, in an effort to cut out the middleman," Nona said.

"And I knew the cop was up to something and had to be in on it when I saw the giant bulge in his pocket . . . not drugs!" she crooned.

SASSY SENIOR SLEUTHS MYSTERIES

4

CALIFORNIA ADVENTURE

P.C. JAMES

KATHRYN MYKEL

CALIFORNIA ADVENTURE

Mini Mystery #4

Pauline yawned, hiding her open mouth discreetly with her brochure. The tour bus driver had been prattling on all day and she had no interest in the history of medieval weapons, the inner workings of the actors' union or his dry murder puns. She'd never much cared for movies, and now, in her seventies, she found them all utterly unappealing, preferring to read a good cozy mystery instead. When Nona had suggested a tour of the homes of Hollywood's greatest stars, Pauline had thought it would be John Wayne, William Powell, Maureen O'Sullivan or Myrna Loy, but it wasn't. It was people she'd never heard of and whose movies she'd never seen.

The bus driver pulled the open air double-decker bus up to the curb. As the passengers exited the bus, he grumbled something under his breath that Nona didn't make out. "What did he say?" she asked Pauline as they stepped onto the curb.

"I don't know. He's not very good. Not that Raúl, the tour guide, is any better," Pauline said as the guide ushered them towards the front door of the weathered three-story Victorian Tudor.

This latest house, nice though it was, reminded her of the Cluedo game. The interior was as one would expect of a home from the 1900s, with dark wood paneling from floor to ceiling, and it was sparse—the library (unused), the conservatory (unplanted), the drawing room (unfurnished) and so on. She grinned and nudged Nona, who was listening intently to the guide, who finally had something to say that piqued her interest. He described the onetime star's last movie.

Pauline said to Nona, "Can you see a police officer coming through that door and announcing there is a body and telling us we have to guess who, where, and with what?"

"Shh," said Nona, still listening eagerly to the scandal of forty years ago that had ended the star's career. When their guide stopped speaking and asked them to follow him through the door into the kitchen, Nona seemed to realize Pauline had asked a question. "What?"

"I said . . ." Pauline stopped. There was no point in repeating what Nona had missed, so she just said, "It is like the house in the Cluedo game, I think."

Nona looked at the paneled walls and back at Pauline. "You mean Clue," she said offhand, nodding and agreeing. "It is. I agree. Maybe we get to solve a pretend murder at the end. We should take note. Look at those medieval weapons over there." Nona pointed across the room. "Those swords on the wall, they'd be a perfect murder weapon."

"Or the old Winchester right here." Pauline laughed, getting into the game. "It would be good to end the tour on a mystery. If not, we must suggest it to them."

"I think it's a great idea, as long as it is a fake murder mystery.

I was really looking forward to not having to be in the middle of the action on this trip," Nona said.

"I remember the guide saying at the start of this . . ." Pauline was about to say something uncomplimentary when there came a stifled cry from the room they were about to enter, and the line of bodies ahead of them came to a sudden stop, causing Pauline to shuffle to the side to avoid a collision.

Nona giggled. "Here we go!"

Pauline groaned inwardly. It had better be a quick case, she thought, or they might have an actual murder on their hands. Her feet ached, she was hot and tired from trailing around and she hadn't heard of any of these 'greatest stars' throughout the whole long day.

The line backed up. Nona and Pauline stepped aside to let the other tourists all pass back into the foyer. Their fellow tourists were serious and whispering in hushed tones, solemn as if in church. When the line was out of the passageway, Nona dived into it with Pauline in close pursuit to see what the backup was.

The guide, Raúl, was at the farther end with his arms stretched out to prevent them passing.

"Go back, please, ladies," he said. "There's been an accident in the drawing room and we mustn't disturb anything. The police will be here soon, and then we can carry on to the next house."

Neither Nona nor Pauline moved. They were too busy taking in all the details of the scene inside the room.

"It seems I guessed right," Pauline said. "There is a body and we will surely have to determine who, what and when," she grumbled.

They stood peering over Raúl's outstretched arms. Inside the room facing them, lay a man who'd had a terrible encounter with a rifle. It was so recent, gunpowder still faintly lingered in the air. Scanning the scene, Pauline quickly decided it was not the type of murder she preferred to investigate. Much too messy and quite possibly a suicide or murder made to look like it.

"Ladies, please," their guide said, trying to usher them back down the hallway, "this is no place for idle curiosity."

"Idle curiosity? Don't you know who we are?" Nona asked, bristling at being fobbed off. "We're famous sleuths, and this is a crime scene."

"I'm sure it's just an unfortunate accident," Raúl replied.

"Clearly you're not very observant," Pauline said, turning to go back to the group.

Wailing sirens told them the police had arrived. Raúl looked anxiously through the window. Help arrived in the form of several police officers who immediately began taping off the crime scene, followed by a determined detective.

"Why are those two checking out the scene?" the detective asked Raúl. "This ain't no movie."

Before Raúl could reply, Nona said, "We're detectives, and we've years of experience in crime, especially solving murders."

The detective laughed. "And I'm Cary Grant," he said. "Sorry, ladies, this is police business, and you aren't police. Join the others. We'll talk to you later and you can give me the benefit of your wisdom then."

They did as he asked, fuming with impatience and resentment at his dismissal.

"The butler did it," Nona joked.

"It's never the butler, though, is it?"

"That's why it will be—this time, Pauline."

"I hate to say it, but maybe we should leave this one to the police and continue on the tour. This is too dark, even for me, especially at my age," Pauline said.

NEARLY AN HOUR LATER, the detective let the tourists, now hot and bothered, be on their way.

"Have you ever walked away from a murder mystery?" Nona asked her friend as they took their seats back on the bus.

"Yes, once, when I first got started."

"You know what's been nagging at me? The gunshot. We didn't hear it," Nona puzzled.

"Oh, that is an easy one. I believe the killer left behind a clue," Pauline replied.

"Oooh, what did I miss?"

"A silencer. I would bet this day trip that the murderer used that old Winchester with a silencer."

"Wait, how did you come to that conclusion?" Nona asked.

"The Winchester was on the wall when we left, but it had an addition. The silencer," Pauline said smartly.

"I didn't even know that you could put a silencer on one of those. That detective is going to be sorry he didn't have you on the case, Pauline."

Pauline smiled. She knew she really was good at sleuthing. "Yes, I have seen it in those MyTube videos. Silent as a mouse when fired. It is pretty fascinating. By the way, thank you for sitting on the lower level this time. It was too hot up top."

"Sure. I think you mean YouTube videos." Nona laughed. "You think we should contact the detective and let him know?"

"No. I really do not think he wanted us to get involved. Besides, we will probably solve the case for him before the day is out, anyway."

"We sure make a great team. Where are we headed next?" Nona asked, pointing to the trifold brochure Pauline was fanning herself with.

Pauline unfolded the brochure so both women could get a good look and said, "From the look of the pictures, it is a haunted house."

"Make sense for the last stop. Sounds interesting. Care to wager whether it will be a ghostly murder or another Clue game?" Nona emphasized the word Clue. Sometimes it seemed her friend was stuck in a bygone era.

"You say Clue, I say Cluedo. You know Cluedo is a real thing, I did not just make it up or get it wrong."

"Ooh-kay," Nona said, amused.

"Anyway, I doubt we will get lucky enough to find two mysteries in one day," Pauline responded. "But I will go with ghostly—you can have the Cluedo."

"Lucky? Who are you callin' lucky?" Nona chuckled. "Especially since we walked away from the first one."

Pauline waved off Nona's antics and shook her head. "I don't think that detective would have been amenable to our help, no matter what we offered."

FIFTEEN MINUTES LATER, the bus pulled up in front of an iconic haunted house scene. Dilapidated exterior, a rusty front gate, overgrown weeds and even a cemetery in the rear of the property.

"You win," Nona said, looking at the sight before them.

"I cannot imagine this belongs to some famous movie star. Maybe Freddy Krueger!" Pauline held up the map to read the details. "That is puzzling. It only lists the address. No other details. Now that is a mystery."

"I am impressed at your knowledge of the movies, Miss Riddell, that was a good one!" Nona clapped her hands. "Well, it's the last stop, let's make the most of it." Nona urged Pauline off the bus in front of her.

"If we don't break a leg on the way in," Pauline mumbled under her breath, grabbing ahold of the tour guide for stability.

Once all the tour guests were on the porch steps, he quieted everyone. "Welcome to the Mansion," he said.

"That was anticlimactic," Nona whispered to the woman standing next to her.

The tour guide opened the front door, and Pauline bravely stepped into the foyer.

"Wow, this place is amazing!" a man at the front of the group said.

Nona pushed her way past a few people to catch up to Pauline to see what all the fuss was about. She couldn't imagine anything that looked nice given the creepy state of the exterior.

The tourists filed into the foyer of dark wood paneling and were greeted by a butler. "Ha, I win," Nona said.

"Not so fast," Pauline murmured.

Nona had to admit the decor of this house looked even more like the Clue game than the last. Complete with a creepy waxed statue of a colonel holding a candlestick.

Nona and Pauline were just about to explore when clicking, creaking, and banging came from the walls.

"It must be a ghost story, then," Pauline whispered.

"All part of the show, I wonder?" Nona suggested, giggling at the theatrics of the doors locking and the shutters closing.

"Ladies and gentlemen," the butler began in that deep, measured tone movie butlers always employ. "Welcome to this most haunted of houses. None of its owners lived to tell the tale of what happened here after dark." He let his audience murmur appreciatively, before continuing, "Don't worry, your tour guide Raúl will have you back in the bus before nightfall. Do not hesitate to ring, should you need me." The butler finished his act by ringing a small bell bolted to the wall.

The visitors laughed nervously.

The whole group turned to the left as Raúl took over the tour. "Many of you, I'm sure, will have seen the movies Haunted House, Murder House, It Came at Night, and too many others to list right now. If you have, then you'll recognize some scenes here in these rooms."

"Why are we locked in?" one of the younger tourists asked, a tremor running through his jocular voice.

"It's all part of the tour," Raúl said smoothly. "It's getting you in the right frame of mind to enjoy the horrors we'll see. I'm joking about the horrors, of course."

Pauline confided to Nona, "I really don't like Raúl any more than the bus driver. He's not very genuine as far as his technique as a tour guide."

Raúl finished his speech, "I'll see if they're ready for us to move along the tour." With that, he jiggled the handle for the door to his right. Finding it locked, he tried the door to his left. It opened and he stepped in. There was silence for a moment before everyone began chatting about the movies they'd seen and how this foyer was just as it appeared in some film or other, at which there was instant disagreement, and the chatter grew more animated.

Nona looked over the paintings on the wall. Props, no doubt, painted to look vintage and old-fashioned but with modern cast members, some of whom she thought looked familiar. Before she placed the faces, the door opened and Raúl stepped back into the room, slamming the door closed behind him and leaning against it.

"Ladies and gentlemen," he said, "I'm afraid we're going to be held up here because there's been another suspicious death."

Turning her head away from the man's retching, Pauline

whispered, "That doesn't seem to be an act. He's not faking shock. There must really be a body in that room."

"Two murders in one day," Nona murmured.

"Well, there goes my chief suspect. I was leaning towards Raúl as the number one suspect at the last scene. You remember he went ahead of us?"

"Maybe, Pauline, but he wouldn't have had time to replace the Winchester on the way out before you saw it, because he was behind us then."

"True. And he likely did not kill whoever is in there."

"Or did he?" Nona questioned. "That would be a perfect cover. Pretend like he is going in to see if the other actors are ready. None of us guests would suspect him."

"I have to admit, Nona, I'm disappointed. I had been puzzling it out the whole way over to this property and I was sure I had it. Let's get him outside for some fresh air. Must not be easy discovering two bodies in one day."

"Unless he's the murderer," Nona mumbled under her breath.

"Must be his lucky day," someone said from within the crowd of tourists.

"Lucky?" a woman shrieked.

From the back of the group someone shouted, "How do we get out? We're locked in the foyer!"

"Try the front door," Nona called out, amongst disgruntled murmurs.

"It won't open!"

The rattle of door handles and banging against the doors disrupted the outcries.

"None of them will open," the tallest man yelled over the heads of everyone in the group. "We're locked in!"

As Nona ushered Raúl to sit down on one of the throne chairs next to the wax colonel, she said to Pauline, "This is a new one for me. Have you ever been in a locked room mystery before?"

"No, I can't say that I have," Pauline replied.

"What are we going to do?" a shout came from near the front door. "We're going to die here," the woman said, emerging from the group to stand by Nona and Pauline.

Nona furrowed her brows. That woman is even more theatrical than I am, she thought. "Calm yourself, lady."

"Just use your phone and call 911 for help, please," Pauline urged one of the panicking women standing between her and Nona.

When the woman stared at her blankly, Nona handed the woman her phone and said, "Use mine."

A puzzled look flashed across Raúl's face.

"What?" she asked.

"You, er, can't call 911," he replied.

"Why?" Pauline asked. None of the doors worked, all were locked. The shutters were closed and couldn't be opened from the inside.

"Ah, well, it's part of the show. We jam the signals," he said, shamefaced.

"Is that even legal? Can we turn it off? What do you do in case of an emergency? I don't know what stunts you pull here in the United States but most places that's not allowed!" Pauline questioned.

Raúl said, "I do not know, the butler usually handles it. All I have to do is ring the bell."

Nona pulled Pauline to the corner and whispered, "So the only unlocked door was the one the guide went into, the one that has the dead body behind it. How do you want to play this?"

"I guess we should handle it just like those that came before us. I'll be Miss Marple and you'll be Sherlock Holmes," Pauline said seriously.

"O-o-kay, if you think so. Where do we begin? It's not like there's a manual for how to solve a locked room murder mystery . . . Wait, was there one? Did I miss it?" Nona questioned, clearly out of her element here. She was more of a 'let's run with a wild theory and see where it takes us' kind of sleuth.

Everyone behind them had gone quiet while the two amateur sleuths stood at the far end of the room and talked it out.

Pauline turned and said, "I say it begins with whoever or whatever is behind that door." She pointed a long slender finger towards the closed door. All was silent save for a collective audible gasp from the crowd.

"Wait just a minute," Nona chimed in. "Everyone knows that if we all step into that room, we are all going to get locked in there, or some of us go in, some will get locked in and some will get locked out." Nona raised her eyebrows and imperceptibly put her foot down on the idea. She didn't always get credit for her movie antics and gut reactions, but she knew she was right about this one.

"Okay. You and I will go in and the rest of the group will remain out here." Nona said, nodding to Pauline. They continued their conversation as though there was no one else in the foyer with them.

"No, you can't leave us," a young man said from the crowd. Though eight other people didn't really count as a 'crowd.'

"Alright, let's think this out. We go in, they stay here. Then what?" Nona asked.

Pauline turned to Raúl and scowled at him, "When do they unlock the doors and shut off the jelly phone thing?"

Nona giggled. "Jam the phones, Pauline."

"They don't," Raúl said. "Well, at least not until we make our way through the tunnels and out the back exit to the cemetery. Once you exit from the room," he pointed to the door to his right this time, "there's a mechanism that triggers one door at a time, and once we leave the back exit, all of the doors and shutters will unlock and open, and the phone signal will resume."

"More good news," Pauline said with her hands on her hips. "So we need to go through that door to get out?" She raised her hand and pointed to the door on the right.

Raúl hung his head and said in a barely audible voice, "Yes, the kitchen, but it is locked."

Nona paced along the wall a few feet. "First, our priority should be getting out of here. And since none of us killed the person, I think we are all at risk of the actual murderer. Second, we have to deal with the body. Many of these fine folks are not accustomed to seeing dead people in real life. It will be a shock to them."

Nona turned to Raúl, who was mopping sweat from his forehead, and asked, "Is there anything in that room we can use to cover, hide or store the body with?"

"Yes, of course. It's a coat closet," he said.

Pauline looked up. "We are supposed to escape into a coat closet?"

"No. No. That is where an actor stays during the tour, and then we are supposed to go through the kitchen, which as I said leads to the cellar and out through the tunnels to the backyard cemetery," he whined and shrugged both shoulders. "But we can't open any of the doors, except that one."

"Which is a coat closet?" Nona shrilled.

"Yes."

The rattle of doorknobs, banging on doors, and nervous murmurs filled the room, as panic set in. The tourists were trying in vain to get out of the foyer and escape into one of the other rooms, or out the front door through which they'd come.

Ignoring them, Nona said, "Okay, tell me this." She waited

until Raúl looked up at her. "Who is in the coat closet?" She stared pointedly at Raúl.

"The butler. Of course."

The room fell silent and then was filled with another collective audible gasp.

"The butler—do you mean the man who let us in?" Pauline asked.

"Yes, it was the butler who let the tour in."

"But he only just left us. It's been minutes," Nona said. "Nobody has had time to kill him, have they?"

"Well, they have. If you don't believe me, go see for yourself," he said hotly.

"Definitely dead? Are you sure?" Pauline asked, as she turned the door handle and hesitated.

"He looked as dead as he could be with a battle-ax sticking out of his chest," Raúl said.

"Okay," Nona said. "But this is Hollywood. They have really great props and makeup people here. Are you sure?"

He replied, "It wasn't the butler who was supposed to be dead, and the body wasn't supposed to be in the coat closet, nor covered in actual blood. And that was definitely an actual weapon. I don't think this is part of the show."

"Maybe the actor who was to play the body did not show up," Pauline said. "So, the butler stepped in and the makeup got a bit out of hand."

"See for yourself," he said, gesturing to the door.

With her hand still on the doorknob, Pauline said, "All right, let us do this."

Nona followed Pauline inside. At the sight of the body, she said, "He really is dead." It was very realistic, but not nearly as bad as the last corpse. This is Hollywood Nona thought.

The two sleuths crossed the space of the enormous walk-in closet, nearly the size of a small room.

"Check for a pulse," Nona said, dodging a hanging jacket prop. The body of the butler lay slumped against the wall.

"Very dead," Pauline said as she reached down to check for a pulse, "but still warm. He really has been killed, butchered with the ax, since he let us in."

"Well, we can't walk away from this one," Nona said. "Or the entire city will be dead by sundown."

Pauline replied, "this puts an end to that theory. It seems, once again, the butler did not do it."

"But somebody did," Nona replied. "And this time, we have to find them. If we can't phone the police, it's down to us."

"Oh, good," Pauline said sarcastically. "Two aging amateur sleuths and a posse of twittering tourists against one crazed murderer. What could possibly go wrong? The term 'bloodbath' won't do it justice, if the murderer is still here and we unmask him."

Pauline turned to face Nona and took a deep breath. Nona stood across from her, with the sleeve of a minx coat hanging from the coat rack over her shoulder, and looked at Pauline quizzically. Did she just say posse and twittering? Nona asked herself, and laughed hysterically.

Wiping her eyes from the laughter, Nona said, "Nonsense, it's ten of us against one of him . . . or her . . . eleven if you count the guide, Raúl, if he could actually be useful? Let's see if we can figure out if there is any other way into this room besides the door we came in."

"The murderer got in and out undetected," Pauline said. "So it stands to reason that there must be a trapdoor or secret passageway?"

"The guide said something about a tunnel," Nona replied as she started banging on the walls. "If there was a tunnel leading out from the kitchen, maybe it also leads elsewhere?"

"I bet there is, because if the house was used for movies, they would want multiple exits," Pauline said, pressing on the upper wall panels.

The walls, however, withstood all their efforts and the murmuring of the crowd in the foyer grew restless and louder.

"Now what?" Nona said, as Pauline's face lit up.

"Not the walls," she said, "the floor."

Nona started stomping her feet while Pauline gently got down on her knees and scrabbled at the old wooden floorboards until, with a cry of triumph, Nona said, "You've got it."

"Way to steal my thunder," Pauline said, raising a plank that exposed a handle.

"Careful when you pull that," Nona said, hovering. "We could be standing on the bit that moves, or worse, drops out from beneath us. We had better back up."

Pauline backed up as far as she could while still being able to reach the handle. Nona plastered herself against the side wall and stood on her tiptoes. Pauline slowly pulled the lever upright, and a section of wall slid open to reveal an exit. Pauline crossed the floor, stepping over the plank and lever. Each of them standing on opposite sides of the opening, they peered in.

"I can't see anything, can you?" Pauline asked.

"Not even with my glasses would I be able to see." Feeling for a light switch on the inside of the wall, and half expecting they were going to find an old torch that they would need to light with fire to illuminate their way, Nona said, "A light switch. I've got it." She flipped the switch. A dim yellow glow gave light to a narrow stone passageway and a set of stone steps.

"They must lead down into the tunnel," Pauline suggested.

"Tunnels. Now we know there are two."

"Or one tunnel that is interconnected."

Hesitantly Nona asked, "Are you game to go down?"

"Yes, let's see where it leads, then we can get the others and escape as a group."

"After you, Miss Riddell."

Pauline was just about to step through when Nona said, "Wait."

Pauline stopped. "What is it?"

"That tunnel," she said, pointing to a branch in the tunnel on the left. "It looks like it curves back towards the front of the house."

"That's a good thing, right?" Pauline questioned.

"Well, for one, if it does, then it is possible it would have allowed a murderer to kill the butler and rejoin our party with none of us realizing what we'd seen. And then, two, if we exit the tunnel, what if it is rigged with the same mechanism as the kitchen tunnel's exit? It would trigger the doors and windows to unlock and open."

Pauline replied, "Okay, that is a good thing, also?"

"We need a plan in case we exit and the doors unlock. We don't want the killer escaping again with no one knowing who it is. It has to be someone in our party."

"Yes. I agree with that. After all there can't be two murderers wandering around Hollywood murdering people wherever our group goes." She contemplated. "Or the guide, and I am betting on Raúl. It is logical to suspect that he knows both of the victims."

"And his way around down there," Nona said, waving her hand into the passageway opening.

"If he does this tour often, as he said, he must have at least met them," Pauline said. "We may not know his motive, but he had the opportunity and the means. It has to be him. We can wedge this plank against the door, under the knob, so he can't follow us through."

"Well, he can't hurt us if we exit through the tunnel, but what about the others?" Nona said. "He'll be locked in with the others. What if he panics and takes a hostage? There are some serious medieval weapons on the walls in the entryway foyer."

"Well then, the others can defend themselves with the same weapons," Pauline replied.

"And once we get out, if the doors open, we will be defenseless to stop him. There are no weapons in this coat closet," Nona said, pulling at a coat hanger. "I am not MacGyver." She turned and jabbed the thin metal hanger in the air like a fencing sword to prove her point.

Nona stood, contemplating the plan, and Pauline said, "The bus. The bus driver. Remember, he was telling us about the relics he had. We can get him, and a weapon at the same time."

"Okay, I think we've got a solid plan. I will bring this hanger, though, just in case." Nona laughed. "Let's get this door barricaded behind us."

The two women wedged one end of the plank under the doorknob and the other end against the opening the plank had come out of and set off down the steps. It was eerie and quiet, their footsteps echoing through the tunnels.

As they came close to the exit, Pauline pointed. "I think we're nearing the exit, look." The passageway was brightening.

"I can't believe it's Raúl, though," Nona said as they reached the end of the tunnel. "He doesn't seem to have the stomach for murder. He got faint at the first scene, at the sight of blood."

Pauline was about to reply when a gruff voice said, "Far enough, ladies."

"The bus driver?" Pauline murmured.

The bus driver stood in front of the two, holding a long dagger that shone as the tunnel light pinged off its sleek beveled edges.

"So much for the guide," Nona said sarcastically.

"The others are following us," Pauline said quickly. "You can't hope to kill all ten of us."

"Nice try, lady," the driver said, grinning unpleasantly, "but every word you said echoed down here, and I know you locked them in."

"We did say that," Nona replied, "but we couldn't. It was a coat closet, there was no lock on the door. They will come looking for us soon."

"I'll be long gone before they find the courage to come down those steps."

"What is the plan here?" Nona asked. "Kill a couple of little old ladies? That's brilliant."

"No, officer, I never saw the two ladies. They must have been so scared, they made a run for it. I have been on the bus this whole time waiting for the tour to end, officer," the driver said mockingly.

"You think you have this all thought out, do ya?" Nona said, antagonizing him, and gave a nod to Pauline. Nona darted her eyes up and down rapidly, so Pauline could see, she was fiddling with the coat hanger behind her back.

Taking her cue, Pauline asked, "But why did you kill the two tourists?"

"Ha, those weren't tourists, those two men were undercover."

Pauline and Nona both cocked their heads and said, "Undercover?"

"They were filming a movie this whole time. You may have seen it? Undercover Management."

Pauline looked quizzically at Nona, and Nona shrugged and shook her head.

"They were management for the tour program. The first guy posed as a tourist, and that stiff, up there," he pointed above them, "he was playing the 'butler,'" the bus driver said, irritation in his voice that the two women weren't understanding his grand plan.

"Oh-kay, that explains the who, but still not the why," Pauline said as Nona tried to concentrate on the coat hanger.

"The union, of course. I want the union to come in so we can get better wages, lunch breaks and paid time off. I have been explaining all this to you for the better part of the afternoon."

"Oops, I guess we should've paid more attention to our surroundings," Nona said, smiling a devilish grin. At the moment the driver turned his head to look behind him, Nona launched at the man with her coat hanger extended. She had unbent it to its full length, leaving the hook at the end. It was long enough for them to stay safely away from the man with the dagger, and the hook at the end provided just enough leverage to knock the dagger from his hand. It fell to the ground with a clank and Nona yelled, "Grab the dagger." Then, she lunged and plowed into him, pushing him towards the exit, and he tumbled out onto the ground.

Pauline grabbed the dagger and stood over him with the weapon hovering near his stomach. "Don't move," she said. "Can you get a signal out here, Nona? Call for the authorities."

"I don't have my phone. I left it with the woman inside."

"I AM glad we stopped for breakfast before heading to the airport. All the excitement of yesterday gave me an appetite," Nona said as she spooned a pile of scrambled eggs into her mouth.

Pauline lowered the newspaper just below her eyes and stared at her friend, who was talking with her mouth full. "It says here they were onto the bus driver for some general mischief. They found the Winchester and have plenty of evidence to convict him for both murders. He'll get life in prison."

"I wonder what kind of 'union' he will find in prison." Nona chuckled and raised her hand to her mouth.

"I told you, you should not talk with your mouth full, no matter how hungry you are," Pauline chided. "Well, we might have been wrong about the 'who,' but at least we were right about the second exit being hooked up to a mechanism that unlocked the doors. We didn't need the authorities this time."

Nona laughed. "You are right about that. The look on that detective's face when he saw you bent over the murderer, with that huge dagger—priceless."

5

DESTINED FOR SANDESTIN

P.C. JAMES
KATHRYN MYKEL

DESTINED FOR SANDESTIN

Mini Mystery
#5

Nona and Pauline stood in the warm sand, gazing out to sea. Windsurfers and paragliders raced across the waves and swooped into the air as the gusty wind held them aloft.

"I wish I was twenty again," Nona said sadly. "That looks like fun."

Pauline smiled.

Nona had received an email from a Floridian travel agency with an amazing deal for a five night stay at a brand new resort just minutes from the pier.

Once Nona had assured Pauline that it was not a time-share scam, they agreed to meet there at Sandestin on the Florida Panhandle, a pleasant escape from the end of the north's winter. Though even here, the storms were in evidence. The difference was back home in Canada, or even in Nona's hometown in Massachusetts, the wind was piling up snowdrifts, while here it provided waves for adventure seekers to play on.

"Is your hearing aid buzzing?" Nona asked Pauline.

"I don't wear a hearing aid," Pauline said, appalled at the question. "It must be your own."

"I don't wear one either. That's why I asked if it was yours," Nona said, chuckling.

On a recommendation from the resort manager, they'd left early to enjoy the beach activities before boarding their party cruise. The two long-time friends stood on the beach near the entrance to the pier, awaiting their party boat, Nona dressed in her matching cotton pants outfit, a sweater tied around her neck like a proper Bostonian, and Pauline with a light spring jacket and matching blue capris.

Out at sea, a powerboat tossed up spray as its roaring engines drove it forward. Behind, a young woman rose, slowly at first but then quickly higher, in a brightly colored parachute. Soon she was high in the air. The boat turned to make a run along the length of the horizon, and onlookers gathered on the sandy beach to take photos.

Pauline and Nona strode closer to the surf as the paraglider waved and shouted. It appeared she was shouting to them personally, even though there were dozens of people crowded nearby. They couldn't hear what she said, but she looked as excited as she looked terrified. She was too high, and the noises of wind, waves, and powerboat engines filled the air and drowned out her words.

Pauline gasped in dismay as the girl and harness parted company with the parachute, which now blew raggedly out to sea like a lost scarf. The girl, however, hurtled towards them like a missile, and the two women hurried away from the shore, up the beach, Nona nearly knocking over a reporter in their path.

Behind them, near the water's edge, there was a sickening thud and then horrific screaming from the group of young people who moments prior had been excitedly recording the event, but hadn't the sense to flee.

Nona and Pauline raced back towards the water to the girl, who lay crumpled on the sand. She let out one guttural groan, her eyes blank, staring up at them. Pauline checked for a pulse, but there was nothing to be done for the girl. She closed her eyelids, took off her spring jacket and placed it over the girl's head. Pulling away, she paused, then peered closer. The cords of the harness that once connected to the parachute were partially cut.

"Stay back," Nona said to the crowd of gawkers arriving on the scene. Nearby, the shutter of the reporter's camera clicked wildly. The bystanders grudgingly backed up, their expressions a mixture of horror and naked curiosity. All except one young man, who clearly understood what had happened. His face was ashen, and he looked like he would throw up at any moment.

"The best thing for any of you to do at this point is to call 911," Pauline stated matter-of-factly, directing her words to the sickly man. He was too stunned to react, and it was the crowd who produced their phones and began tapping away at their screens.

"Wait," Nona said. "Only one of you. It'll only confuse the issue if you all call."

After they all stared blankly at each other, wondering who should make the call, Nona pointed to the kid closest to her and said, "You make the call." The decision and the call were made. The group didn't have to wait long. Emergency services arrived within minutes and took charge of the scene.

The police interviewed Nona and Pauline first and released them just in time to get on their party boat excursion.

ON BOARD, Nona eyed her surroundings and her friend curiously. "I thought you said this was a 'party' boat? I think you tricked me. There's an awful lot of beer and fishing equipment on board this boat." Nona put one hand on her hip and waved the other at the fishing gear.

"Well, it is called a party boat. Though I never promised you a 'party,'" Pauline retorted and shrugged one shoulder.

"Are you actually going to fish?" Nona asked mockingly. "Pauline?"

When her friend didn't reply, Nona turned to see what she was preoccupied with. Pauline gripped Nona's arm to get her attention. "Don't look. Isn't that the couple from the beach who continued filming after everyone else started to call 911?"

"Too late, I am already looking," Nona said. "I was really miffed about that. People have no respect for the dead these days! Like that reporter. I am glad you thought to cover the girl with your jacket."

"What reporter?" Pauline asked while still keeping her eyes on the couple intently. As the boat took off, both women put a hand on the railing to steady themselves.

"Eh, just some rando, looking to get his five minutes of fame. There were a lot of eyes on us, and on the scene today. Why is it that everywhere we go, we end up in the middle of an 'accident,' crime or murder?"

"I believe the expression is *fifteen* minutes of fame," Pauline corrected.

"Sure. But do you ever tire of being fodder for their stories?"

Pauline didn't respond.

Nona snapped her fingers. "Pauline . . . Florida to Pauline!"

"Nona, what are you prattling on about? I was lip-reading their conversation."

"Oh, sorry, carry on." Nona turned to watch the scene. "Wait, what are they saying?" she whispered.

"I think it was 'upload the footage by five o'clock, and check the bank account for the deposit.'"

"Pauline, you need to call the authorities. It's possible those two were responsible for that poor woman's death."

"You call them," Pauline said. "You're the one with the phone."

"You have to get a cellphone, Pauline. You can't function in the modern world without one."

"You make the call," Pauline said, "and I will talk. I will describe the two culprits and tell the police what I think I saw them saying."

AFTER SEVERAL HOURS on the boat, with Nona and Pauline taking turns keeping a close eye on the suspicious couple, the boat returned to the dock. The police were waiting and the two elderly sleuths pointed out the suspects exiting behind them. The police wasted no time placing the suspects in cuffs and driving the pair off to the station.

"I think that's our quickest solution yet," Nona said and grinned, showing her complete set of pearly white false teeth.

"I'm sure it is," Pauline said. "How foolish of them to discuss it where anyone could have overheard them."

"They weren't near anyone, and you only 'heard' them

because you're good at lipreading," Nona quipped. "Why are you anyway? Good at lipreading, I mean."

"I was near an explosion once," Pauline said, "and it left me deaf for weeks after. I learned the skill quickly, as you can imagine."

"Danger and intrigue. Tell me more," Nona squealed and clapped her hands repeatedly. "Was it something to do with a case?"

"It was," Pauline replied, and related the event as they walked the few blocks back to the resort.

THEIR SPIRITS WERE high when they got back to their resort. The vacation was finally looking up when the concierge gave them free tickets to a show that another guest had left behind. The ladies enjoyed an evening's entertainment in a neighboring resort, but they came down to earth with a bump when Nona's phone rang. She answered it, and her stomach dropped as she listened intently. Her face molded into a deep frown. Pauline shook her head in mock annoyance at the disturbance of their enjoyment of the show.

"Well?" Pauline asked, when Nona disconnected the call by closing the flip phone.

"It wasn't them," Nona said. Her face bore a pensive look. "They're just a couple of callous people who knew they could get rich off their video. They've sold the rights to it, to one of those national TV stations."

"So much for 'our quickest solve ever,'" Pauline said, completely deflated.

"We'll sleep on it tonight and have the answer by morning,I am sure of it," Nona said, more brightly than she looked. As exhilarating as it was to be in the middle of the action, the business of solving crimes at their age was also exhausting.

THEY ARRIVED BACK at their suite after nine to find the evening edition of the local newspaper tucked under their door.

"Anything good?" Nona asked, kicking off her shoes and rubbing her feet, as Pauline sat on the nearby sofa to read it.

"Oh my," Pauline replied. "We're on the front page . . . and it isn't a very flattering picture."

Nona walked to the couch and sat next to her to get a good look. "Foolish reporter, taking a picture of two old ladies . . . like that! What is this gossip rag, anyway?"

Pauline replied, "The Daily Tracker," and pointed to the newspaper's name above the article.

They both agreed, neither the night nor the morning had brought any new ideas at all. They sat companionably, nibbling breakfast in the kitchen nook in their multi-room suite.

"It has to be someone she knew," Nona said. "Someone who had a grudge maybe, or someone who benefited from her death."

"It could also be a mistake," Pauline said. "Maybe she got the parachute meant for someone else. She's too young to be worth killing this way."

"Not if she's the daughter of a billionaire and she has a sibling who now inherits everything," Nona speculated.

"She and everyone else on the beach looked very ordinary," Pauline said. "I think billionaires' kids would be on private islands, not here at Sandestin."

"It's coming up on spring break," Nona said. "She could be here from a university."

Pauline shook her head. "I still think it is a grudge or a mistake. Were there any others going up at the same time?"

"I don't remember any," Nona said.

"So most likely a grudge," Pauline said. "Or a prank gone horribly wrong."

"The prankster thought she'd fall harmlessly in the sea, you think?"

"I do," Pauline said excitedly, "and that just gave me a clue. I think I know who did it!"

"Who?"

"When everyone was losing their heads with the phones and crying, and not knowing what to do," Pauline said, "there was one young man who was white as a ghost. He just stood there gaping. I bet he was the boyfriend."

"I remember now," Nona said. "Tall, gangly kid, with ginger hair. But usually you leave the wild speculations to me."

Pauline nodded. "That's him," she said. "Do we phone the police again or investigate this theory ourselves?"

"Investigate," Nona said. "They'll be upset if we send them on another false trail."

"Okay, let's go, then," Pauline said, wiping her mouth, rising quickly and placing her napkin on her plate. "Some of the gawkers could be on the beach right now. We can interrogate."

"They're teenagers," Nona said. "You won't see them on the beach till after lunchtime."

NONA WAS RIGHT. Pauline walked and watched the beach all morning, but not one of the gang from the day before appeared until after the two women had finished their own lunch.

"There he is," Nona said, "and doesn't he look sick?"

"A guilty conscience if ever I saw one," Pauline agreed. "You would think he would stay away. People seeing him like that will suspect him at once."

Nona said, "He probably thinks if he stays away, people will be even more suspicious."

"I don't think anyone but us noticed the harness was cut," Pauline said, "but you're probably right. Let's question him first."

"What questions?" Nona asked her overly excited traveling companion. "Excuse me, did you murder that girl yesterday?"

"We'll ask if he knew her, that's all," Pauline said, hurrying over to where the young man stood, slumped against a railing on the pier, staring out to sea.

"We saw you yesterday," Pauline blurted, when she drew close enough to talk, "at that awful accident. Did you know the poor young woman?"

"Smooth, Pauline," Nona mumbled.

The twenty-something nodded. "I'm to blame," he said, his voice hoarse and trembling. His whole body sagged and his expression was agonized.

"Should we tell the police?" Pauline asked in a raised voice, signaling behind her back to Nona what she thought was the international hand gesture to *call the police*.

He shook his head. "They wouldn't understand," he cried out, his despair replaced with a growing agitation, and his body became rigid.

"I am sure it was just an accident," Pauline said, and took a step back. She turned her head slightly and breathed a sigh of relief, seeing Nona was definitely on the phone.

"An accident," he snarled. "That's what you think? I should never have done it. Everyone was egging her on. I, I . . ." He stopped, unable to continue. His eyes fastened on Nona, who had her phone to her ear, and he ran towards the sea.

"Stop him," the two women called at the same time. Two

men at the water's edge looked up at their shouts and sprang into action. A very creditable football tackle, Pauline thought, brought the kid down.

BY THE TIME the police had arrived, however, the two sleuths had already wormed the entire story from the boy. When her friends had gone up on the parachute, the girl had said it terrified her to do it. Some had offered five or ten dollars, not enough to persuade her, so, eager to impress the girl, this guy had offered a much larger sum because he knew she couldn't resist doing it for her favorite charity. That had clinched it. Without him and his money, he had told them while sobbing through the entire story, she would never have gone up there.

The police agreed to take him away to a clinic for his own safety.

"He just needs counseling," the officer in charge said to Pauline. "Lucky you two were here or he could have killed himself."

When the police had gone, Nona said, "Well, that was half a win."

Pauline nodded. "But it leaves us no further forward. I don't remember anyone else acting strangely."

"I am thinking this was just an awful mistake. The wrong person got into that harness," Nona replied. "Poor girl."

The pair made their way back to the shuttle bus and back to the resort, heads down, deep in thought the whole way.

SITTING at the small two-person table in their suite, something about the case just didn't feel right with either of the women.

They knew of no motives for cutting the cords to rig a murder, and they had eliminated the obvious suspects close to the girl. So, what was left? What was the common thread?

Could it have been an accident, as the authorities claimed, or even just a coincidence? Was it plausible that the two friends were vacationing here and just happened to be on the exact beach at the exact time a girl dropped from the sky?

Nona knew in her gut there was no such thing as coincidence—especially in investigating murder mysteries. She had learned that lesson early in her days with the CIA.

So there had to be a clue somewhere, and they had missed it. Something that would explain the cut cords, and how Pauline and Nona came to be on the beach to witness the death.

"It's us!" Nona blurted out as Pauline poured the tea. Her outburst caused Pauline to flinch, and she spilled some of the tea on the fine white tablecloth.

"What is this all about? What is *us*?" she asked, wrinkling her eyebrows and giving Nona a quizzical look.

Nona explained what she had been thinking. "The common factor is 'us.' Someone killed that girl to get at us, or at the very least staged a murder to get our attention."

"If you think that has merit, we will need to revisit everything we thought we knew about the crime, from the beginning and with a fresh perspective," Pauline replied. "It certainly would explain the chills and the eerie feeling that someone has been watching us."

"You didn't tell me you felt that way!" Nona drank her tea. "Okay, let's think about it from the beginning. The hearing aid. When I started hearing strange noises."

"I told you I don't wear a hearing aid," Pauline chirped back at Nona and raised her eyes wide behind her cup of tea. She sipped from the delicate china. "Seriously now, I think you need to go back further."

"How much further? I doubt the boy in my third-grade class had anything to do with this."

"I said *seriously* now," Pauline chided. "Go back to *why*, or better yet *how*, we just happen to be here right now."

"In this hotel suite? The manager was sweet on you, Pauline, you know that. He upgraded us to a 'more spacious suite on the first floor, overlooking the gardens,'" Nona said, mocking the manager's fake French accent.

"No. Go back further, but do not forget that very important clue. We will come back to that."

"Hmm . . ." Nona pressed her knobby index finger over her lips. "The email we received with the magnificent offer to come here to this new resort?"

"Yes. If you think someone was doing this for our benefit, I think we need to start there. Do you agree?"

"Our benefit? Certainly not, and it wasn't for the young lady's benefit either," Nona scoffed.

"Okay, let us start there. You received an email with an offer that was too good to be true."

"But we are here, aren't we, so it was true."

"Yes. Who could have made that happen? Someone on the resort staff, perhaps. The unsavory manager . . ." Pauline took that train of thought and trailed off.

"I see . . . I didn't buy into his fake Canadian accent," Nona said. "Hmm. He conveniently upgraded us to this spacious suite overlooking the gardens." Nona jumped out of her seat. Well, maybe 'jumping' was a slight exaggeration. She crossed the room quickly, heading for the sliding doors to the gardens.

"What do you see?" Pauline asked when her thought train had arrived back at the station.

Nona looked out. No one was about, and all was quiet. Too

quiet, she thought. She looked down at the handle to open the sliding door. Sand was scattered on the floor—on the inside of the room. Nona stood contemplating this foreign invader. *That is strange.* They hadn't used this door, and Pauline had made it her mission to check that they locked it every time they left the room.

Something buzzed in the distance, but Nona continued puzzling over the clues. Housekeeping wouldn't have used this door or left sand behind. The sand had to have come from the beach because there was no sand in the garden. It looked like a foot. A sandy foot. Footprints, plural, across the carpet. She followed them back towards Pauline, her eyes finally trailing up to Pauline's horrified face. A barefoot man held something up behind her friend. Nona couldn't see if it was a knife or a gun. She instinctively put her hands up.

"Hey there, mister. Let's not get crazy," she said, and Pauline shot her a look that could kill, as the intruder jammed Pauline in the back with whatever he was holding as a weapon. Pauline flashed her eyes downward repeatedly as Nona took in the scene. Must be a signal for Nona to look at what? The table. Nona scanned the scene on the table from their afternoon tea. Her eyes darted quickly between the table and the man. A rope lay beside the tea tray. Nona flashed her own look of horror back at Pauline. *He means to tie us up, or worse. I can't let that happen.*

We've trained for this, you got this, Nona told herself. *This guy isn't even going to utter a breath before I take him down.* She prepared to spring into action.

"Stop right there," he said, not even trying to hide behind his fake French-Canadian accent this time.

Okay, one breath and one sentence is all this creep is going to get. She looked at Pauline, who was blinking her eyes rapidly. *Oh goodness, she's having some kind of seizure.* Her eyebrows were doing a choreographed dance with her forehead as well. *Oh right, Morse code?* Nona groaned inwardly. *Come on, Pauline, I am seventy years old; you are going to make me try to remember Morse code? Just mouth it to me, already . . .* She resigned herself to her fate. *Okay, I guess I need to let him speak so we can stall long enough for me to decipher her code.*

"What do you want, monsieur?" Nona asked the crazed fool holding her dear friend hostage.

Long blink, short blink, short blink followed by a long blink . . . *Agh, pay attention, you old git, your friend's life depends on you.* She focused as Pauline continued the code.

"Lady, I am going to need you to back up and go out through those doors," he demanded calmly.

Lady? Who is he calling a lady? I am a weapon! A Morse-code-deciphering weapon—what was that last one, agh! She'd forgotten she was supposed to be watching Pauline's eyes for the code. She waited for it to start again. Long blink, short blink, short blink followed by a long blink. **Tea.** *Okay, now we are getting somewhere.* Nona stared intently.

Three long blinks, pause, one long blink, one short blink. *Yup, I got it, 'Tea.'*

"What are you looking at?" the man asked, pushing his weapon into Pauline's back again. Nona kept watching Pauline. *'On.' Got it. 'Tea on' . . .*

Three quick blinks and two long blinks . . . *Numbers, why did she have to get into the numbers? I am going to go with a guess of* **three.** *That makes the most sense.*

Sweat was dripping from Pauline's brow. *Now or never.* Nona nodded imperceptibly at Pauline and said, "Tea for three, shall we?" Then she paused: one Mississippi, two Mississippi, three . . . and Pauline ducked. And Nona froze. *A gun. Okay, worst possible weapon.* They both stood there, stunned. The Frenchman had the weapon trained on Nona now.

In a lightning-fast move, Pauline knocked the gun from the

man's hand. A shot whizzed over Nona's head as she bent to grab the teapot. Nona threw the hot tea at his face, hitting him in the head with the teapot too. As the man screamed and clutched at his face and head, Nona rushed to Pauline's side, grabbed the rope off the table, quickly tied a handcuff knot and then tossed it to her friend, who had already taken the man down with her famous groin-kick maneuver. *That had to hurt!*

Pauline was now sitting on a chair atop the man, his hands clutching at his junk, his arms disabled by the rungs of the chair. *Dang, who knew she could still move that fast?* Nona grabbed the gun from the floor and trained it on the Frenchman.

"I got him now," Nona said and plopped into her own chair, still aiming the gun at the man, with her finger firmly on the trigger, safety off. She put her hand over her heart. Her pulse was racing faster than was safe for a woman her age, and she needed to get control of it. "Holy, wow . . . That was awesome!" she finally said to her friend with a big grin.

"Awesome? What are you, twelve? That was scary!" Pauline said. Her first spoken words since the ordeal started. "Keep that gun on him. I need to sit and get my blood pressure under control." She took the chair off the culprit and sat. After a few minutes, both their tickers were pacing normally again. Pauline kneeled to tie his hands up with the rope, all the while threatening his nether region. Nona sat in the chair and continued her 4-7-8 breathing technique.

If I'm not careful, I'll put myself to sleep!

"I think it's time to find out what this creep has been up to. I mean, besides trying to scare the bejesus out of two little old ladies." Nona chuckled.

Pauline used her best interrogation techniques on the man. He was no match for her. Nona watched in amazement while she rang the police.

By the time the police finally arrived, the manager had told the women he had been in love with Pauline since he saw her in a news article after their last case in California. They had been all over the news and even made international headlines—only because Pauline was from Canada, but still.

He'd researched and found that each of the hotels had boomed with business after the women had solved the cases. He confessed to planning this elaborate scheme to get them here, though he hadn't intended on killing the poor young woman. Just some unsuspecting lug-head. But he hadn't cut the cords enough for it to break on the first few boys.

Pauline and Nona recited back to the police what the stalker had done, starting with the email to Nona. He'd known she was the better bet to bite on the deal.

"Why? Why did he go through all this trouble?"

"Well, it is obvious he has a few screws loose, and has some stalker tendencies with this business about love at first sight and all." Nona shook her head. "But he said it was ultimately to gain attention for the new resort. He figured he could drum up attention by having two high-profile"—she paused to embellish the story—"*distinguished* crime solvers staying in his new resort."

"Well, that didn't work out the way he planned," the detective said.

"Nope, the reporter he hired double-crossed him. Instead of doing a puff piece about the two sleuths, the reporter printed the salacious photo of the dead girl and the 'unsuspecting elderly women who just happened to be nearby.'"

"And what about the noises you were hearing?"

"It was his walkie-talkie," Pauline said. She pointed to the man's belt.

"EVEN AFTER ALL THAT has happened, this turned out to be a really enjoyable trip," Nona said, before biting into her breakfast sandwich. "It's too bad we have to head home today."

"It was quite pleasant after the authorities took over the case," Pauline agreed. "You still have not told me about the boy in your third-grade class."

"Oh, that? It was nothing, really. Just a couple of third graders and a missing cat. A cat caper, you might call it. It was that very adventure that ignited the spark for me," Nona replied with a gleam in her eye.

SASSY SENIOR SLEUTHS MYSTERIES

6

A CHRISTMAS CAPER

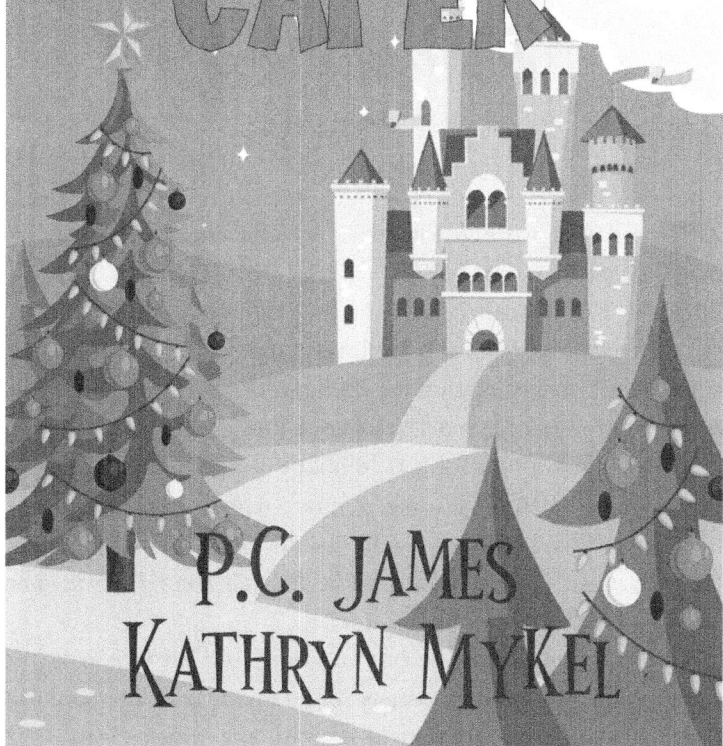

P.C. JAMES

KATHRYN MYKEL

A CHRISTMAS CAPER

Mini Mystery #6

"I'm glad we chose to drive." Nona commented as she stared out the window.

"You mean 'chose a driver,'" Pauline corrected.

"Always proper, Miss Riddell. Yes. I enjoyed the coastal view. If you would have gotten your nose out of that newspaper, you might have enjoyed it, too!" Nona chided.

"I was looking for an article about our last case. I want to know what that meddlesome reporter wrote about us? It was bad enough they caught us with our derrieres in the air in The Daily Tracker." Pauline lowered the Florida Herald newspaper and eyed her friend.

"We're supposed to be on 'vacation,' but all we do is get caught up in solving crimes and mysteries. I'm looking forward to a nice, uneventful trip to 'the most spectacular place on earth.' Especially since it's nearly Christmastime."

Nona nodded her head, daring the universe to produce a distraction.

"Here it is. I've located the article." Pauline scanned the article, her eyes darting back and forth as she read. "There's no mention of us solving the case."

"That's rude! Let me see."

"Rude, indeed." Pauline bent forward and passed the newspaper across to Nona. "This really is more like a limousine than a hired car. I don't know how you always manage all these 'extra perks' for us."

"Trust fund." Nona winked. "I'm glad I didn't fire that travel agency, after all. Otherwise, we'd be flying. In coach!"

They both snubbed their noses at that idea.

Nona folded up the paper and put it on the seat next to her. "Nope, nothing about the two dames who actually solved the case. But I saw an article about 'the most incredible place on earth.'"

"Which is it? The most spectacular or the most incredible?"

"Both, though technically for us, it is 'the most incredible' since we're only going to the Mystic Kingland."

THE NEXT MORNING, the two vacationers stood in line at the entrance to the amusement park. "I don't understand why they need my finger scanned," Pauline argued.

"Don't worry, I read the scan is discarded immediately. I don't fully understand it, but it sounded legitimate. Something about converting the image into a numerical value . . ." Nona trailed off as they approached the turnstile. Nona placed her thumb on the reader and nothing happened. "It's not working. You try," she said as she stepped aside for Pauline.

Pauline placed her thumb on the scanner, and nothing happened.

"Try the other thumb. Push against the turnstile," Nona said impatiently.

"I did, it won't budge."

"I hope this has nothing to do with the incident in the hotel lounge last night." Nona stepped back.

"I doubt they would deny us entry because of that," Pauline was saying, when two park employees appeared out of nowhere.

"Ma'am, you'll have to come with us," they said simultaneously.

"This must be a mistake. We have done nothing. We haven't even made it into the park yet," Nona was arguing when the employee placed his thumb on the scanner and Pauline passed through the turnstile.

"Hey, don't leave me here," Nona whined and pushed through behind Pauline, nearly knocking into her when she stopped short.

"Would you tell us what this is all about, please?" Pauline stood, unmoving.

The taller man said, "You are Pauline Riddell and Gretta Galia, aren't you?"

"Yes, we are," the two women said in unison.

"We're going to need you to come with us," the other man said, gesturing for Nona to move forward. "There's a situation that we're going to need your help with."

The two travel companions looked at each other, puzzled.

"You two are infamous," he said, pulling out a rolled-up newspaper from his pocket. He opened the paper and handed it to Pauline. "You're on the front page."

Gawking at the awkward picture of themselves on the cover, "The Inquirer," Pauline exclaimed indignantly.

"It's a tabloid!" Nona scoffed. "I knew that stunt was going to come back to bite me!"

Both parks employees tried to hide their smiles. The bearded one said, "Seems they have a reputation." While the other said, "You solve crimes, don't you?" They both tried in vain to usher the two ladies further into the park.

"Yesss, we solve crimes. What is it this time?" Nona asked.

"I can't go into detail here," the younger man said. Finally getting the two women to move, he rushed them down Main Street. Just past the Ye Olde Christmas Shop, the man ducked under a tree branch and entered the tree. Pauline stopped abruptly and looked at Nona, who shrugged, and they followed reluctantly. Inside the tree and down a single flight of stairs, the four of them stood in a tunnel. The entire circumference of the tunnel was painted orange.

"Ladies, this is the *Cortility*," the man behind Nona said. "The corridors for utilities that are used by a significant number of the park staff. Cast member services, waste removal, deliveries, and food storage and preparation."

"Our chief of security has turned up dead. Come. Please."

"What does that have to do with us?" Pauline asked suspiciously.

"We'll make it worth your while, if you solve this and keep the police from making it into a federal case," he said.

"Comp our entire stay," Nona said, "and free meals too."

"Sure," he said. "You close this quietly and we'll treat you to a royal stay.

Nona looked at Pauline, who nodded in agreement and said, "I think you have a deal. Lead on."

THE BODY of their security chief lay on its back in an awkwardly splayed out position. The man appeared to have been hit by a truck and thrown against the pillar the body now rested beside.

"Are there vehicles down here?" Pauline asked, puzzled.

"Not usually," he said. "Only electric carts, like golf carts, mostly. We will bring in an ambulance to pick up the body, though, when you're done with it."

"I thought something larger than a golf cart had maybe hit him," Pauline suggested.

The man shook his head. "There've been no trucks down here today. Anyhow, when you look closer, you'll see there are no signs of a collision. No cuts, scrapes, nothing."

"What about powerful fans?" Nona asked. "Could something like that have blown him against this pillar?"

"There's the usual AC and ventilation systems but nothing to blow over a man of Bill's size."

He had a point, Pauline thought. Bill was a burly man and looked to be twice her own size and weight. He couldn't have been knocked over like this easily.

"When did it happen? Were there witnesses?" Nona questioned.

"Nope," he said. "The doc found small marks, but he couldn't be sure they have anything to do with the murder at all. He estimated Bill was killed some time between midnight and 3 a.m. That's the third shift. There were maintenance workers here last night, and we've called them in to question them. This specific corridor isn't used very often by the everyday park staff. So far, no one has admitted to being down here at the time Bill must have been killed."

"It was likely one of the maintenance crew, then," Pauline said, "if no one else could be down here and also have the equipment to do something like this."

"Are there CCTV cameras?" Nona asked.

"There are, but they were out for, you guessed it, maintenance," the man said.

"Then maybe it was one of them," Pauline said. "Who else could take out the cameras?"

"Do you want to interview them all?"

"We sure do," Nona said. "How many of them are there?"

"About forty," he said, "but not all would have been working here last night. Many are groundskeepers and such."

"Then only the ones who work with heavy equipment and who know their way around down here, and those that have access to the security system also," Pauline said.

"To start with," Nona added.

As it turned out, they narrowed it down to only three maintenance workers and one security guard who could have been in the tunnels overnight. One maintenance worker, a shifty man, ill-at-ease and inclined to be hostile to the women, seemed to Pauline to be the most likely murderer. He knew heavy equipment and was openly known to dislike the security chief. His answers to their questions were as evasive as it was possible to be.

Outside of their makeshift interrogation room, Pauline said, "It's him, I am sure of it."

"Then we'll have our private investigator check him out," the younger security man said.

"Hey," Nona cried. "Why are *we* doing the detecting if you have someone already hired to do the work?"

"The private investigator is good for legwork," he said, dismissively, "but not so much for brain work. At least, that's what Bill thought."

Pauline asked, "Did Bill hire him?"

"Yeah, but he had no choice. The investigator is some relation to one of the ladies in the executive offices."

"Then we have someone else who may have a motive," Nona said. "Not just the maintenance guy."

"If you're looking for motives," the man said, with a harsh laugh, "you have a long list of characters. In security you don't make many friends, not with all that goes on around here."

AN HOUR LATER, the private investigator returned to them with his findings. The maintenance man had an alibi for the entire shift. He had been working with another employee, fixing a ride on the other side of the park.

"If he had an alibi, why was he so evasive?" Pauline said, puzzled.

"He runs a small scam and was afraid you'd latch onto that," the detective said. "I'm just waiting for him to slip up big one of these days, and I'll nail him on all the petty stuff. I haven't been able to narrow down who his accomplices are yet, they are always in costume."

"I would think that is something the authorities should already be aware of," Pauline commented offhand.

Nona harrumphed, "Back to square one. Let's eat."

SITTING in a booth that resembled a brightly colored cartoon space capsule from the 1960s, the two women discussed the case over chocolate milkshakes at Granny's Galactic Goodies.

"It is possible it could be the waste collection workers, and we have yet to interrogate the rest of the security personnel," Pauline speculated.

"I doubt it's the waste collection employees. My money is on his disgruntled staff in the security office."

"Okay, what do we know? No signs of hit-and-run trauma, no physical wounds except for some minor burns? And the likely suspect had an alibi," Pauline said.

Nona sucked on her shake straw, making a slurping noise when she got to the bottom of the cup.

"The shake was a pleasant treat, but with free meals, you could not have picked a place with actual food?" Pauline questioned.

"Dessert first," was all Nona said.

After a long pause of contemplation, Nona broke the silence and said, "I read they have this automatic vacuum system for the waste collection. Maybe you are onto something. Maybe it *was* them."

"I don't know how that could have killed the man, especially the way his body was positioned in the Cortility?" Pauline replied.

Shrugging, Nona said, "Yeah, I guess you are right. Do you have any other theories?"

"Sadly, no. Maybe we should head out and enjoy the park," Pauline responded.

"Yes, a ride on Space Cliff should provide some inspiration."

"You do realize that is a rollercoaster . . . completely in the dark?" Pauline scoffed. "I think there is an *age limit* for those rides."

"Pishposh!" Nona uttered as she stood up to leave. "Well, we already saw the mice and most of the princesses. What would you like to do?" she asked and handed the park map to Pauline.

"A trip to Tomorrowville is in order. Maybe we will get a glimpse of the future that will help us solve the case today."

A huge grin washed over Nona's face, and she clapped her hands and said, "That's perfect, we can ride the speedway."

"Remember what happened last time you drove . . . the dune buggy."

"Yes, that was one of our first cases together! Aww, who knew you were so nostalgic, Pauline."

ON THEIR WAY TO TOMORROWVILLE, the ladies were stopped by a crowd of parkgoers huddled around an actor dressed as Buzz Lightwave, who was sprawled out against a tree.

Pauline gave a side glance to Nona with a knowing look. "A second victim," she whispered. The crowd stood silently, gazing at the body. One man in the crowd, in workday clothes and with what looked like a tool bag, seemed familiar.

"We have to do something," Nona whispered in reply. "It isn't safe here with a maniac loose."

"Why do you think it is a maniac?" Pauline asked.

"Because there's no sensible link between these two people," Nona said. "One was a security guard in the Cortility. This one is a costumed actor, just a kid . . . and he's above ground."

"What if they are linked, and we just do not know how yet?" Pauline said.

"We don't have a team of detectives to find a link," Nona reminded her.

"I have a link," Pauline said.

"What?" Nona said.

"Look at his neck," Pauline whispered. "Those look exactly like the marks on the security guard."

"Like a vampire got them," Nona said satirically, but she could see that Pauline was right. Did the park feature vampires? She thought not.

"And look," Pauline whispered, nudging Nona and gesturing

surreptitiously towards the man in workday clothes who was slowly walking from the scene.

"Who is it?"

"The shifty guy we questioned earlier at the other crime scene," Pauline said. "And now he is at this crime scene, too. We need to stop him from getting away."

They set off at a brisk pace until Nona said, "Wait!"

"What?"

It was Nona's turn to surreptitiously gesture to another man, also slowly backing away from the scene. "That gun-thing stuffed inside his jacket. I bet that's what caused these marks."

Pauline thought quickly. Did they choose one man and risk it being the other, or split up and chase each? Individually, they were no match for either of the men, who looked like tough customers. Together, they might.

"We follow the man with the bulging jacket," Pauline said.

They trotted as quickly as they could, hoping someone from security would appear before he spotted them, for they were soon closing in on the man. Their footsteps were loud on the concrete, and he looked back and spotted them, and picked up the pace. Now they were jogging in their effort to keep up.

"I can't go on much further," Nona gasped.

"Nor me, but we have to stay with him until we find help," Pauline stammered out between breaths.

Just when they thought they'd have to give up the pursuit, one of the security men they'd talked to earlier appeared from a doorway.

"Stop him!" Nona cried out.

The security guard took a second to grasp the situation and then stepped right in front of the fleeing man, who reached into his jacket and pulled out a strange bulky pistol. He pointed it at the security man, who immediately backed away. Nona and Pauline crashed into the back of the man, and staggering briefly from the shock, he toppled forward, landing face-first on the asphalt. The gun gave a thump and a bolt of lightning seemed to shoot across two arcs at its top. Then the security guard was on the stunned man. He wrenched the gun from his grip, tossed it aside, and cuffed the perpetrator.

"Thank you, ladies," the security guard said. "I think you saved my life."

THE NEXT DAY, the two sleuths were in the security office with the director of security, the vice president of the park, and the local police chief.

"It's a weapon the folks at NASA have been testing," the police chief said. "It seems our guy is part of a ring of not-so-petty crooks who steal from all the big companies around here. One of his colleagues got it from the Kennedy Space Center. It's a new space weapon, an update on an old-fashioned stun gun, that NASA has been testing."

"Why was he killing people here, though?" Nona asked.

"We don't have a confession yet," the police chief said. "He ain't talking. Probably too scared to. Looks like he felt the heat, and was rubbing out the people here who knew of his crimes. I suspect the two victims were in the crime ring. He was cleaning up loose ends."

"What about the guy with the alibi? The one we didn't chase?" Nona asked.

"Yes, we've arrested that man and the PI as well. The PI made up the alibi and was downplaying the whole thing to keep management off their trail."

"That's pretty risky. What about the relative in the executive office?" Pauline asked.

"Yes, we got her too. She was the mastermind behind the criminal enterprise. Once we arrested one, they all fell like dominos. We might never have tied the entire operation together. How did *you* figure it out?"

Nona looked at Pauline, who said, "We didn't know the 'how.' We were just lucky enough to see him trying to sneak away from the second victim and saw the peculiar-looking weapon inside his jacket. So we knew the 'who.'"

"Well, it was excellent spotting and quick thinking," the parks director said. "I think the deal was that the rest of your stay here is on us. How do you feel about extending that another week?"

The vice president said, "I think you two might even get a tour of the NASA facilities when they get this little toy back."

Nona shuddered visibly at the thought of the space weapon.

"We are on our way to Tomorrowville," Pauline said thoughtfully. "I think we glimpsed the future, and I don't like the look of it. Maybe that rollercoaster that you mentioned, Nona, would be safer?"

READ SASSY SENIOR Sleuths Return

READ MORE SASSY SENIOR SLEUTHS MYSTERIES

Sassy Senior Sleuths Return

Leave a review!

★ ★ ★ ★ ★
5 stars

"I'm going to share it with all my friends!"

"So much cozy mystery goodness!"

Thank you for reading our book!
We appreciate your feedback and love to
hear about how you enjoyed it!

Please leave a positive review letting us
know what you thought.

THANK YOU! × × ×

ABOUT THE AUTHOR KATHRYN MYKEL

Kathryn Mykel, author of Sewing Suspicion - A Quilting

Inspired by the laugh-out-loud and fanciful aspects of cozies, Kathryn Mykel aims to write lighthearted, humorous cozies surrounding her passion for the craft of quilting.

Kathryn is an avid quilter, born and raised in a small New England town. She enjoys writing cozy mysteries and sweet, clean romances.

For more fun quilt fiction cozy reads and new releases, sign up for her newsletter or join her and her Readers on Facebook at Author Kathryn Mykel or Books For Quilters For more quilt fiction in the Sweet Romance Genre you can find her on Facebook at Author Kathryn LeBlanc or on her books on Amazon.

- Newsletter signup: https://view.flodesk.com/pages/ 618e6d793a0e5bcf6f541be1
- Bookbub https://www.bookbub.com/profile/kathryn-mykel
- GoodReads Page: https://www.goodreads.com/ author/show/21921434.Kathryn_Mykel
- Website: https://SewingSuspicion.mailerpage.com

Quilting Cozy Mystery Reads on Amazon:
Sewing Suspicion
Quilting Calamity
Pressing Matters

Threading Trouble
Quilting Sweet Romance Reads on Amazon:
Quinn: Runaway Brides of the West
Christmas Star Cottage

ABOUT THE AUTHOR P.C. JAMES

P.C. James, Author of the Miss Riddell Series

I've always loved mysteries, especially those involving Agatha Christie's Miss Marple. Perhaps because Miss Marple reminded me of my aunts when I was growing up. But Christie never told us much about Miss Marple's earlier life. When writing my own elderly super-sleuth series, I'm tracing her career from the start. As you'll see, if you follow the Miss Riddell Cozy Mysteries over the coming years.

However, this is my Bio, not Miss Riddell's, so here goes with all you need to know about me: After retiring, I became a writer and, as a writer, I spend much of my day staring at the computer screen hoping inspiration will strike. I'm pleased to say, it eventually does. For the rest, you'll find me running, cycling, walking, and taking wildlife photos wherever and whenever I can. My cozy mystery series begins in northern England because that was my home growing up and that's also the home of so many great cozy mysteries. Stay with me though because Miss Riddell loves to travel as much as I do and the stories will take us to many different places around the world.

- Facebook: https://www.facebook.com/ PCJamesAuthor
- Bookbub: https://www.bookbub.com/authors/p-c-james
- Amazon Author Page: https://www.amazon.com/P.-C.-James/e/B08VTN7Z8Y

- GoodReads Page: https://www.goodreads.com/author/show/20856827.P_C_James
- Amazon Series Page: My Book
- Miss Riddell Newsletter signup: https://landing.mailerlite.com/webforms/landing/x7a9e4

Books on Amazon:

In the Beginning, There Was a Murder

Then There Were ... Two Murders?

The Past Never Dies

A Murder for Christmas

Miss Riddell and the Heiress

Miss Riddell's Paranormal Mystery

The Girl in the Gazebo

The Dead of Winter

It's Murder, on a Galapagos Cruise

Printed in Great Britain
by Amazon

36192541R00067